P9-CEA-630

Western District Conference

LOAN LIBRARY

North Newton, Kansas 67117

Call Number
WJ
398.2
Co   r

Date Received 1979

Accession Number
6360

Fund Ed. Com

6360

WJ
398.2
cor

ROUND ABOUT
AND LONG AGO

C-1974

124p. illus

ROUND ABOUT AND LONG AGO

Tales from the English Counties

retold by Eileen Colwell

Illustrated with lino-cuts by Anthony Colbert

HOUGHTON MIFFLIN COMPANY BOSTON 1974

Library of Congress Cataloging in Publication Data

Colwell, Eileen H
  Round about and long ago.

  SUMMARY: Twenty-eight stories gleaned from the
oral traditions of various English counties.
  1. Tales, English. [1. Folklore--England]
I. Colbert, Anthony, illus. II. Title.
PZ8.1.C73Ro4   398.2'1'0942   73-21962
ISBN 0-395-18515-7

TEXT COPYRIGHT © EILEEN COLWELL 1972
ILLUSTRATIONS COPYRIGHT © LONGMAN YOUNG BOOKS 1972
ALL RIGHTS RESERVED. NO PART OF THIS WORK MAY BE
REPRODUCED OR TRANSMITTED IN ANY FORM BY ANY MEANS,
ELECTRONIC OR MECHANICAL, INCLUDING PHOTOCOPYING AND
RECORDING, OR BY ANY INFORMATION STORAGE OR RETRIEVAL
SYSTEM, WITHOUT PERMISSION IN WRITING FROM THE PUBLISHER.
PRINTED IN THE UNITED STATES OF AMERICA
FIRST PRINTING V

CONTENTS

The North Country

East Anglia

The Midlands

The South and the West

For Una
who has heard so many
of my stories

Almost all the stories in this book have been retold from collections of folklore made in the period between 1840 and 1900 from oral tradition. I have tried to retain the directness and flavour of the original while at the same time telling the stories in a more modern idiom so that present-day children may enjoy them as did their ancestors so long ago.

EILEEN COLWELL

THE
NORTH COUNTRY

Cheshire

THE WIZARD OF ALDERLEY EDGE

Once upon a time a farmer was riding from Mobberley, across Alderley Edge, to Macclesfield where he hoped to sell his horse. It was autumn and the skies were grey and a thin misty rain was falling. As he rode along, the farmer planned what to do with the money he would receive. He was sure that he would be paid a good price for his fine snow-white mare.

Suddenly, as he rode past a spot known as Thieves' Hole, a dark shape rose in his path. It was a very tall old man dressed in a long black cloak. The farmer could scarcely see him in the rain.

"Stop!" cried the stranger in such a commanding tone that the farmer reined his horse at once. "I know where you are going and why, but you need go no further. I will buy your horse from you."

"How much will you give me?" asked the farmer, for he liked to make a good bargain.

The stranger named a price, but the farmer thought it too little, so he picked up the reins and said, "I can get a better price than that. I shall go to Macclesfield."

"You will not get a better price for you will not have an offer from anyone, mark my words," said the stranger. "I tell you that you will meet me here this night on your way home and you will be glad to sell your mare to me."

The stranger stepped back and seemed to disappear. One moment he was there, a dark shape in the rain; the next moment he was gone.

The farmer rode on, wondering who the stranger could be. How did he know that he was selling his mare? The farmer felt uneasy but, when he reached Macclesfield, he forgot his troubles for the town was lively and full of people.

The fair was in full swing. There were clowns, quacks selling wonderful medicines, all kinds of stalls and, of course, the horse fair. Confidently the farmer offered his snow-white mare for sale, showed her paces and how sound she was. Men came up and looked her over but, to the farmer's dismay, no one offered to buy his horse. He lowered the price but still no one made an offer. The farmer could not understand it at all. What was wrong? Could it be anything to do with the mysterious stranger?

At last, as it grew dusk, the farmer set out for home again. At first he thought he would not go over Alderley Edge for he did not want to meet the stranger again. But in spite of himself he found he was riding up to the ridge after all.

"At least I shall get something for my mare," he thought, "even if it is not as much as I hoped. I need money for the rent."

The meeting place was beneath a great rock near seven tall fir trees. The farmer rode more and more slowly as he drew near the lonely place. It was so gloomy and quiet! Sure enough, the tall stranger was waiting against the rock, his dark cloak round him and his face in shadow.

"Lord save us!" thought the farmer. "The man might be a robber. I should be wise and ride away before it is too late!" But he did not move, for he was too afraid.

The stranger stepped forward and said, "Follow me. You shall have your fair price." Shaking with fear the farmer obeyed.

Then began a journey the farmer never forgot. The old man led him over wild heathland, through leafless woods, by Stormy Point and Saddle Bole. The farmer, leading his horse, stumbled after him in the dark. Scratched by brambles, bruised by rocks, he grew more and more frightened.

At last the stranger stopped before a great rock cliff. He seemed to grow taller than ever. His cloak billowed round him as he drew a wand from beneath it and waved it several times in the air. The farmer saw great iron gates where there had been none before and he heard a horse neigh underground. Thunder rolled and the gates swung open. The farmer knew, too late, that the stranger was no ordinary man but a wizard. His horse reared up on its hind legs with terror and the farmer cried, "Spare my life and you may have my mare!"

"Do not be afraid," said the wizard. "Enter boldly and you shall see a sight which has never been seen by mortal eyes before."

He went through the gates and the farmer followed, leading his mare. They came into a great cave, as large and lofty as a church. From the roof hung crystals which gleamed and sparkled in a mysterious light. Everywhere were men in armour but they lay asleep on the ground, their swords and spears at hand. Their steeds lay beside their masters and each horse was snow-white in colour. Not a sound could be heard and the sleepers did not stir although the farmer's footsteps echoed through the cave.

In the innermost cave were heaps of coins and precious stones and here the wizard paused and said, "Help yourself to a fair price for your mare. I need one snow-white mare, so I must have yours."

"Who are these men and why do they sleep here?" asked the farmer in a whisper, for he did not dare to speak loudly for fear of waking the sleepers.

"They are warriors who lie asleep until a day when they must awake and descend to the plain to save their country in a great battle. Never again will you or any man see me or the iron gates. Go home now in safety."

The wizard led the farmer through the caves to the iron gates. As he passed his mare he saw that already she had sunk to the ground in an enchanted sleep.

Thankfully the farmer passed through the gates and they shut behind him with a clang which echoed among the hills. He turned; nothing was to be seen but the dripping rock. The gates had disappeared. A horse neighed deep down beneath his feet and then there was silence.

When the farmer reached home and told his tale, few believed him. One or two men looked for the iron gates, thinking greedily of the treasure behind them, but no one could find the place again.

The warriors still sleep with their horses beside them until the time comes for them to ride forth to save their country.

Lancashire

THE ENCHANTED FISHERMAN

One night a fisherman was in his boat in Morecambe Bay. It was nearly midnight and a mist was rising. He was just about to sail for home when he heard a peal of bells which seemed to come from under the water. He leant over the side of the boat to listen better and when he raised his head the mist had cleared and the moon was shining.

To his surprise he did not recognise the country round about. There were mountains but not the mountains he knew; there was a beach near at hand but not the one where his cottage stood; he was near the mouth of a river but it was not the River Kent. Although his sail was down, his boat moved along quickly as if drawn by a current. Presently it grounded in a small cove he had never seen before.

The fisherman jumped ashore. A strange green light shone over the countryside, not at all like moonlight. Nothing looked familiar.

Then there was a sound of music and a crowd of little people dressed in green ran towards him, dancing and singing. One of the little men reached up and took hold of the fisherman's finger and tugged it as if inviting him to follow.

"These people must be Greenies!" thought the fisherman. "They are so small that there can't be much harm in them." He had often heard of the Greenies—a kind of fairy—but he had never caught sight of one before.

The little people led him through a wood to the entrance of a cave. The light was so dim and green that the fisherman could not see a step before him, but he felt mossy stones beneath his feet and saw a gleam of light ahead.

He came out into an open space ringed round with flowers. It was smooth and green, a fairy ring, and hundreds of Greenies were dancing there. The music of the unseen musicians was so gay that the fisherman himself joined the dancers. He capered about in his clumsy way until he was so tired that he fell to the ground and slept.

When he woke the Greenies had gone and he realised that he was very hungry. "How I wish I had something to eat," he sighed. Immediately a feast appeared on the grass before him. He fell to at once for it was not often he had a chance to eat such rich food.

"I wish I knew where I was!" he said. At that very moment he saw a beautiful little Greenie. She was so lovely that he forgot his own rosy-cheeked wife and gazed at the fairy in wonder at her beauty. He felt sure that this must be the Queen of the Greenies, and so she was.

"You are in the land of the Greenies where it is always day and where everyone is happy," said the Queen. "While you are here, you are my subject and must obey me."

"I want nothing better," said the fisherman, but before he could pull himself to his feet, the fairy Queen had vanished. He ran into the wood, but although he searched for hours, he could not find her. Sometimes he heard mocking laughter but he saw no one and the strange greenish light never changed.

Whenever he was hungry he had only to wish and food appeared before him. "Why shouldn't I have other things I need?" he thought. "I wish for plenty of money," he said aloud. Almost before he had finished speaking, many gold pieces fell in a shower about him. He filled his pockets and then took off his boots and filled them too.

"Now if I could find my boat again, I could go home and be a rich man for the rest of my life," he thought. He began to make his way through the woods in what he hoped was the right direction. After a time he came to the fairy ring again. The flowers round it were fox-

gloves and in every one a Greenie sat, swinging to and fro very contentedly as the wind blew. The beautiful Queen was sitting on a mushroom while some Greenie tailors stitched a cloak made of moths and butterflies' wings in brilliant colours. At the Queen's side stood the King of the Greenies. He was wearing a suit of burnished beetle wing-cases and a hat with a crimson feather.

Delighted to see the lovely little Queen again, the fisherman knelt down and kissed her hand. Immediately a host of Greenies attacked him. They pinched him with their tiny hands and pricked him with their needle-sharp swords and pulled every hair he had on his head. The fisherman flung out his arms wildly to beat them off, but he was so large and clumsy that the little people evaded him easily, laughing mockingly in their reedy voices. At last he was in so much pain that he shouted desperately, "I wish I were safe in my boat in the Bay!"

Immediately he found himself in his boat, rocking gently on the tide. The moon was shining but now with its familiar soft light.

He hoisted the sail and drew in to Poulton beach where his cottage stood.

He went in and crept into bed. Although his adventures had seemed to last so long, it was now only just past midnight.

In the morning he told his wife of his adventures but she laughed at him for dreaming such strange dreams.

"But it wasn't a dream!" protested the fisherman. "See, I have brought back a fortune!"

He put his hand in his pocket—but it was empty. His boots stood by the hearth, but there was no gold in them. Search as he might, not one coin of the fairy gold remained!

"You see, it *was* a dream," said his wife, laughing.

His friends laughed at his strange story too, but secretly many of them looked for the land of the Greenies, although always in vain.

As for the fisherman himself, he could not rest. Again and again he searched for the lost magic land. One moonlit night he sailed away once more and this time he did not come back.

Perhaps he found the land of the Greenies after all—who knows?

THE DEVIL'S BRIDGE

In Westmorland, at Kirkby Lonsdale, the broad river Lune flows through a beautiful valley. There are steep banks and beech trees and the water in the river is clear and sparkling.

A fine bridge crosses the river, well built but so narrow that walkers have to take refuge in recesses in the parapet when there is any vehicle on the road. Children love to stand in these nooks for there is always something to see from the bridge, especially when there has been heavy rain. The water may bring down anything from a tree trunk to a boat which has slipped its moorings.

The bridge has a strange name. It is called the Devil's Bridge and this is the story of how it got its name.

23

Long, long ago there was no bridge over the river. People crossed by a ford, a part of the river shallow enough to wade through. But when the flood water came down in bad weather, no one dared to cross for fear of being swept away and drowned.

One night when it was pouring with rain, a farmer's wife stood on the Kirkby Lonsdale side of the river looking anxiously across to the other bank. Her husband had waded through the ford in the morning to see that all was well with his sheep on the other side of the river. Now it was growing dark and the water was so high that he might be drowned if he tried to return.

A friend joined the farmer's wife. "Dear sakes!" she said. "How will your man get home tonight?"

"I hope he doesn't try," said the farmer's wife. "If only someone would build a bridge here for the likes of us—I wouldn't care who it was, even if it were the Devil himself."

There was a clap of thunder. "Done!" said a voice and there was the Devil, cloven hoofs, whippy tail and all, grinning all over his ugly face.

The women were terrified. The farmer's wife was the first to get her wits back. "Thank 'ee, sir," she said. "But when will you build the bridge?"

"This very night," answered the Devil, "but there is one condition."

"And what's that?" asked the farmer's wife boldly. Her friend crept nearer to her for comfort and stared at the Devil's twitching tail.

"You must promise me that I shall have the soul of the first live thing to cross the bridge I shall build," said the Devil cunningly. He knew quite well that the farmer's wife was expecting her husband and that if there were a bridge the farmer would certainly cross it, however strange it might seem to find it there.

Well, the farmer's wife had to agree. What else could she do? She went to her home nearby determined to think of some way to outwit the Devil. And she did!

The Devil was true to his promise. As soon as it was dark he began to fetch stones and rocks and drop them into the river to make a foundation for the bridge. It was a terrible night. The rain poured down, the lightning flashed without a pause, thunder roared. The Devil swished through the air, dropping the stones with a rumble and a splash and the noise was so terrible that everyone—except the farmer's wife—put their heads under the bedclothes in terror.

The farmer's wife watched what was happening from her window. She could see the dark figure of the Devil rushing to and fro, his arms full of stones. Then he began to build the bridge and very strong he made it because of the wide, swiftly flowing river. Then he built three arches to carry the footway. At first the bridge was only wide enough for one man to cross, then for a man with a wheelbarrow, and then for a cart and horse.

Faster and faster he worked, hurtling through the air, piling the stones on one another and fastening them together with great splashes of mortar from his sharp trowel. Busy as he was, he shouted with triumph every now and then as he thought of the man's soul he would gain because of his night's work.

But even the Devil could not complete so great a task in one night. Just as he was carrying a great load of stones across the fells, he heard a shrill "Cock-a-doodle-do!" It was a cock on the farm crowing to let everyone know that the dawn had come. With a howl of rage the Devil dropped his armful of stones on to the fells and there they lie to this day.

The farmer's wife came out of her house. The rain had stopped and the sun was shining on the fine new bridge the Devil had built. It stood many feet above the swollen river. The farmer's wife knew that her husband would soon be coming to see if he could cross by the ford.

"Well, I've done it!" said the Devil, switching his tail proudly.

The farmer's wife looked across the river. She could not see her husband yet. "Thank 'ee, sir," she said. " 'Tis good of 'ee."

"What about my reward?" asked the Devil. "I've done my part of the bargain."

Again the farmer's wife looked across the river. Her husband was coming over the brow of the hill with Bess, his collie dog, at his heels! "You've done well," she said to the Devil. " 'Tis a fine bridge . . ."

"My reward! My reward!" said the Devil getting impatient. "Where's that husband of yours?"

"He'll be here soon and you shall have him," said the woman, her hand in her apron pocket. Her husband was walking down the bank and had stopped in amazement at the sight of the bridge. She must hurry with her plan or the Devil would see him.

The Devil's whippy tail was moving so fast that she could hardly see it. "*Give me my reward!*" he yelled, and at the same moment the farmer's wife threw something to the middle of the bridge and called, "Bess! Bess! Here's a bone for you."

The dog bounded on to the bridge to fetch the juicy bone she had thrown.

"There's your reward," cried the farmer's wife. "The first living thing to cross the bridge. Take it and be off with you."

The Devil turned to see who was coming just as the dog ran to greet its mistress, the bone in its mouth. The dog ran between the Devil's legs and tripped him up. The farmer, running across the bridge, gave him a kick into the bargain.

There was a bellow of rage that was heard for miles, a flash of lightning and a smell of sulphur, and the Devil disappeared, never to return.

And that is how Kirkby Lonsdale got its bridge—so the story says.

THE WIZARD OF
LONG SLEDDALE

There was once a man called Doctor Lickbarrow who lived in Long Sleddale in Westmorland. It was a small dale and everyone knew Doctor Lickbarrow, but they did not *like* him for strange things went on at his farm. The Doctor was bad-tempered and when he stared at children from under his heavy black brows, they ran for their lives. His servants were afraid of him and when he passed even the dogs growled and slunk away with their tails between their legs. There was certainly something strange about Doctor Lickbarrow.

"He's a wizard, that's what!" people whispered behind his back.

Wizard or not, one fine still day in September Doctor Lickbarrow decided to go to church. No one sat by him, however, and the congregation paid him more attention than they did the preacher.

The service went on as usual until suddenly a tremendous wind sprang up and howled so loudly that no one could hear the parson talking. Slates were blown from the church roof and branches of trees whirled past the windows. The people were terrified, but not Doctor Lickbarrow. He got up, walked calmly down the aisle and out of the door, and set off for home. He guessed that the Devil had something to do with the storm and therefore with him.

It was a wonder that he was not killed on his way, for trees crashed on either side of him and flying branches narrowly missed his head. Nothing harmed him and he walked along steadily, swinging his cane and humming to himself as though he cared little for the storm.

At the gate of his farm one of his farm servants met him. He was in a dreadful state, covered with mud, dripping wet and shaking with fear.

"What's the matter?" asked the Doctor.

"Eh, sir, everything is the matter! The cows kicked me into the muck; the goat butted me into the duck pond and the dogs and cats seem to be right mad—"

At that moment the farm cats rushed past them, their fur on end, their mouths open in a frantic mew. They were followed by a hen with its skirt of feathers blown inside out and a fat pig that ran so fast it fell over its own trotters with a squeal.

"The Devil must be here as I thought," said the Doctor and he hurried into the house.

Doctor Lickbarrow kept his Book of Magic in the parlour. The book was so powerful with the magic that was in it that he chained it to the desk so that no one could take it away and make mischief. Now as he looked into the room he saw that his apprentice, a young lad, had opened the book and was standing there, his hair on end, unable to move for terror. His hand was fast to the page and, looking over the boy's shoulder, the Doctor saw that the book was open at a page headed, "How to raise the Devil."

Without a word, his master seized the lad, tore him away from the book and threw him out of the door. Then he took the book into his hands and tried to close it. It was a terrible struggle for the book seemed to have a life of its own. The fire burnt with a blue light, there was a loud explosion and smoke filled the room. A haystack blew past the window and a slate crashed through the roof upstairs. At last the Doctor succeeded in slamming the book shut.

At once there was complete silence. The haystack settled down where it was, the hens stopped clucking, the animals stood still, shaking on all their four legs but alive. The Devil had gone; the hurricane was over.

There was no more trouble from the Devil for a long time, but the Doctor's apprentice left in a hurry for a safer job!

THE CUCKOO
OF BORROWDALE

Borrowdale is a very beautiful valley in Cumberland, but in winter the sun is only seen there for a short time each day. Sometimes the snow is so deep that no one can come in or out of the valley for weeks. The streams and the waterfalls are frozen hard and a bitter wind howls up the valley.

Spring, when it comes, is very welcome. The streams thaw, there is blossom on the hawthorn trees and primroses and bluebells bloom on the banks and in the woods. All day long the cuckoo calls across the fields.

Everyone is happy in the spring and would like it to last as long as possible. So one year the people of Borrowdale said, "Why should the spring go away? The cuckoo is the bird of spring. If we can keep it here perhaps spring will stay too."

"But how can we keep the cuckoo here?" asked a little boy, for children are always asking questions.

There was silence. No one spoke for a time, for no one knew what to say. At last an old man said wisely, "We will build a wall across the dale and then the cuckoo will not be able to fly away."

What a splendid idea! Everyone was delighted and the men of the village began to organise the building of a wall at once.

The wall was to be built across the narrow entrance to the valley where the hills came down on either side. The men loaded stones in their wagons, the women wheeled them in their wheelbarrows, even the children carried a stone each. The men built the wall without mortar, as they do in the north of England, cleverly laying stones on top of each other in such a way that the strongest wind could not blow them down.

The men worked, the women brought them food, the children played at "We are the Roman soldiers", and the sheep stared at them all with their silly faces.

It took a long time to build the wall, but the weather in May and early June was good. The sun shone, the wind blew and everyone grew sunburnt and healthy with the long hours in the open air.

Each day the wall grew higher and longer. Each day the cuckoo sang its song, *Cuckoo, cuckoo.*

"Sing on, cuckoo," said the old men. "There is plenty of time for you are going to stay with us always."

"But grandpa," said a little boy, "the cuckoo has wings. Won't he fly away?"

"Not when we have finished this wall," said his grandpa and everyone laughed kindly at the silly little boy.

At last the wall was finished. The cuckoo was safely shut in. Everyone was so tired that they fell asleep just where they were.

Early next morning the people woke. Now they could go on with their work in the fields and the women could clean their neglected homes. Now it would always be spring.

"But grandpa," asked the same troublesome little boy, "where is the cuckoo?"

Where indeed? Suddenly someone cried, "Look!" The cuckoo was flying through the air *outside* the wall singing mockingly *Cuckoo! Cuckoo!* A last faint *cuckoo* came to them as the grey bird flew towards the south and there was silence.

The people watched the bird out of sight and then turned to look at their wall.

"What a pity we didn't build it one stone higher," they said, "for then the cuckoo couldn't possibly have escaped!"

And they went home to breakfast.

Northumberland

THE ENCHANTED PRINCESS

Once upon a time, in the great castle of Bamburgh in Northumberland, there lived a beautiful young princess called Margaret. Her mother had been dead for many years and Margaret had been her father's housekeeper ever since. Now the King was to marry again and had gone to fetch his bride. Margaret's only brother, Childe Wynd, was away seeking his fortune across the seas, so Margaret was alone in the castle except for the servants.

At last the day came when, from the battlements of the castle, she saw a band of knights riding along the road by the shore. At their head was her father and in their midst rode her new mother with her ladies and men-at-arms.

Margaret ran down the steps to welcome her father. Then she

turned to the new Queen to welcome her too. When they saw Margaret the Queen's pages said to each other in low voices: "This princess of the north is surely more beautiful than our princess from the south." Unluckily the Queen overheard what they said and was very angry, for she could not bear to think that anyone could be more beautiful than she was herself. She was filled with jealousy of her step-daughter and began to think how she could get rid of her.

That night a feast was held in the old castle and Margaret laughed and danced with the young knights. No one was gayer than she and, when at last she said goodnight to them all, she looked forward to another day of pleasure. Her ladies helped her to prepare for bed and then left her to sleep.

The next morning the princess had disappeared. Her bed was empty. The King, her father, fell ill with grief when no trace of his dear daughter could be found. His knights rode far and wide but they could find no trace of her.

"Why grieve for her?" asked the Queen spitefully. "She was jealous of me and has run away to some hiding place. She will come back when she has got over her temper."

The King could not believe this of his daughter, but he ceased to speak of his loss. In time it seemed as though the princess was forgotten.

Nobody knew that the Queen was a witch and that it was she who had sent the princess away. On the night of the feast she had used her spells to make everyone fall into a deep sleep. Then she had gone to Margaret's room and changed the poor girl into a hideous monster and driven her out of the castle into the forest.

Soon people began to tell stories of a terrible dragon that was to be seen in the countryside. It breathed out fire and burnt crops and haystacks and set fire to cottages. At night it wandered through the fields like a column of fire. The bravest men could not kill it for its skin was covered with strong leathery scales.

THE ENCHANTED PRINCESS

The hiding place of the dragon was a cave at the foot of a steep cliff in the forest called Spindleston Heugh. Those who lived near this place moved away and left their homes and fields to fall into ruin. Outside the cave, however, there was a large hollow stone and it was found that if this was filled with milk every day, the dragon stayed quietly in its cave. Each day, while the dragon slept, brave men brought the milk of seven cows and poured it into the hollow. As soon as their pails were empty, the men ran away as quickly as their legs would carry them.

Far away across the sea Princess Margaret's brother, Childe Wynd, was told by travellers of the happenings in Northumberland. He was distressed when he heard of the frightful dragon and the strange disappearance of his sister whom he loved dearly. He vowed he would go home to search for his sister and kill the dragon.

Childe Wynd called his men together and they built a fine ship for the voyage. The mast was made from the wood of a rowan tree so that it should be proof against witches and spells; the sails were of the finest and strongest silk; the bows were covered with shining silver. In this ship Childe Wynd and his men set sail for home over a calm sea. After a long voyage they saw the shores of England once more and the square tower of Bamburgh Castle.

The Queen sat alone in the castle. She had no companions except her ladies-in-waiting, for the King was away at the wars. All day long she studied her books of magic. She knew that the only person who could harm her was Childe Wynd and he was far away across the sea. But one day she opened her magic book and read there that Childe Wynd was approaching.

Hastily she climbed to the top of the tower and looked out to sea. A fine ship was skimming across the waves towards her. Childe Wynd was coming home.

Filled with anger, she called up a band of witches to whip the sea into a storm. The witches stood on the cliff waving their skinny arms and shouting curses. The wind blew with hurricane force, the thunder crashed and the waves rose up like mountains in the path of Childe Wynd's ship. But the Queen's spells had no power against him.

Then she sent the soldiers from the castle to attack the ship, telling them that it belonged to pirates. Because of her spells the soldiers believed her. They did not know that the ship carried their young master, the King's son, so they attacked him and many of them lost their lives. But the men had no power against Childe Wynd.

Now the dragon came down to the shore. It spread its great wings, blotting out the sun, and breathed out fire and smoke. Childe Wynd and his men turned and fled. In her castle the Queen laughed with triumph.

Childe Wynd sailed farther down the coast and ordered his men to anchor at Budle Sands. There he waded ashore and set out alone to find and kill the dragon. He pushed his way through the forest, hacking away the brambles from his path until he was very weary. At last he came to the dragon's cave and saw from the tell-tale whiff of smoke coming from it that he had found the dragon's home. Bravely he called to the monster to come out and fight him.

It did! What a terrible sight it was! Its fiery breath scorched him as it rose into the air; its wings cast a dark shadow over Childe Wynd and its glowing eyes shone like fire so that the prince had to shut his own to escape the glare.

"Back, monster!" cried the prince. "If you attack me, I shall cut off your head."

To his surprise, the dragon did not try to attack him. Instead it flew nearer and spoke to him in a gentle voice. "I will not harm you," it said. "If you love your sister still and wish to see her alive, put away your sword and kiss me three times."

The prince shuddered with horror. What, kiss this dreadful monster! How could he do such a thing? He put away his sword, for this he knew he could do safely, but he did not do what the monster asked.

The dragon spoke again. "If you dare not do as I ask, your sister will be lost to you for ever. This is her last chance to win back her own shape."

The dragon's voice was so sad that the prince believed what it said. He knew that, however terrible it seemed, he must do as the dragon asked. He stepped towards the dragon and he kissed it three times. The earth shook, thunder roared and there was such a bright flash of lightning that the prince cowered down and shut his eyes. When he opened them again, the dragon had disappeared and there stood his long lost sister, as beautiful as she had ever been.

Full of joy, the prince and his sister went home together. At the gate of the castle stood their father, back from the wars. He wept with happiness to see his daughter again for he had thought she was gone from him for ever.

The wicked Queen was standing at the King's side. As soon as she saw that the Princess Margaret had regained her own lovely shape, she knew that her power was over. Stealthily she crept away in the shadow of the wall of the castle, hoping to escape.

But Childe Wynd was watching and he ordered the soldiers to seize her. As they held her fast, he used his own magic powers to end her wickedness. Before their eyes the Queen grew smaller and smaller and became a scaly toad which hopped away to wander for ever on Spindleston Sands.

And the princess and Childe Wynd, her brother, and the King their father lived together in happiness for many a year.

Durham

THE FAIRIES OF MIDRIDGE

It was August and the harvest had been gathered in at Midridge in Durham. The last load was brought into the stack yard. Now the men who had worked so hard through the long summer day were enjoying the Harvest Feast provided by their master, the Lord of Midridge Hall.

As they sat drinking ale from their pewter pots, the men told stories of ghosts and witches and fairies.

"Aye, and there are fairies on yon hill," said one man. "My grandam has often seen them."

"Rubbish!" said Willy, one of the young men. "There are no such things as fairies."

"What, no fairies!" came a chorus. "You're daft to say such a thing." One man said, "I reckon you'd not dare to go up the hill and call aloud:

> Rise little Lads,
> Wi' your iron gads,
> And set the Lad o' Midridge home."

"That I would," said Willy, for he had had so much ale to drink that he cared for no one.

Off he went to his master's stables, borrowed one of his horses —without asking if he might—and rode off to the hill, watched by all the harvesters.

He rode quickly at first, then the silence of the night and the darkness sobered him a little. An owl swooped by and startled his horse
so that it reared and nearly unseated him. He almost turned back but
at that moment the golden harvest moon rose from behind the trees
and he saw that he had reached the foot of the hill.

He stood up in his stirrups and shouted into the darkness:

> "Rise little Lads,
>   Wi' your iron gads,
>   And set the Lad o' Midridge home."

No sooner had he said the words than hundreds of the Little
People swarmed round him, pinching and beating him unmercifully.
Their King led the attack, a sharp spear in his hand as long as a
knitting needle. Fortunately the plunging of the horse spoilt the
King's aim, or Willy would have been killed. As it was he fell off his
horse and was almost smothered by the crowd of fairies.

Then the King cried:

> "Silly Willy, mount thy filly,
>   And if it isn't well fed,
>   I'll have thee before thou gets home to bed."

Willy clambered on to his horse and rode for home as fast as he
could. The hunt was up! The fairies streamed after him, some flying,
some running, and all of them tormenting him. Some swung on his
horse's tail and others rode on its back, so that the maddened animal
galloped like the wind.

So loud was the drumming of the horse's hoofs and Willy's yells
for help, and so wild was the screaming of the fairies, that the Lord of
Midridge and his servants rushed out to see what was happening.
Realising the danger, the Lord of Midridge ordered the servants to
open the doors of the great hall.

The entrance was both high and wide. Willy rode straight into it, scattering the fairies in every direction. He pulled up his horse a few inches from the long oak table and the servants crashed the doors together and swung the stout iron bar across them.

Willy fell off the horse's back, more dead than alive. He trembled so much that he had to be supported to a bench and given a drink to revive him. The horse stood, its sides heaving, steam rising from its hot body. Outside the howling of the fairies died down and all was still. But no one dared open the doors until morning light gave them courage.

When they were opened, it was found that the King's spear, small as it was, had pierced right through the iron-studded oaken doors. The strongest man in Midridge, the smith, had to use all his strength to pull it out again.

Never again did Willy mock at the fairies and never again did he go near the fairies' hill after dark.

THE MYSTERIOUS TRAVELLER

L ong, long ago on the shores of a lake called Semerwater near Wensleydale in Yorkshire, there stood a small town. The people who lived there had money and land but they were selfish and greedy.

One day a poor man came walking through the town. It was October and the lake was grey and ruffled by the cold wind. It would soon be night for the end of the day comes early in the dales.

The traveller had a pack on his back. He shivered in his thin clothes. He knew he must find shelter for the night, but he was sure that someone would take him in.

43

A man was standing at his open door, the firelight glowing behind him. "Could I have a bed for the night, friend?" asked the traveller.

"We want no strangers here," growled the man.

A few cottages farther on, a woman was watching for her husband to come home from work. The traveller was about to ask if he might shelter there but the woman shut the door in his face.

It was the same everywhere; no one welcomed him. At one house the dogs were let loose and he had to run; at another the wife called for her husband to set about him with a stick. In the street a horseman crowded him off the road so that he was spattered with mud. Even the children gathered at the street corner, jeered at him and threw stones.

Tired and hungry, the traveller walked on until he had left the town of unkind folk behind him. He came to a small, grey stone cottage standing by itself. It was so small that it seemed to be tucked into the hillside for shelter. A twisted hawthorn tree hung its scarlet berries over the steep roof.

"Perhaps I shall have better luck here," thought the traveller and he knocked at the door.

It was opened by a cheerful looking little woman wearing a spotless white apron. "Come you in," she said at once. "You look cold and clemmed."

"Thank you," said the traveller gratefully. By the hearth sat an old man. A kettle steamed on the hob and a black cat lay asleep on the mat.

"Sit you down," said the old man. "You're welcome to anything we have. 'Tis good to have a visitor. Folk round here are not friendly."

The traveller shared their supper of oatcakes and milk and when it was done he lay down near the fire, for there was only one room. The wind howled outside but within the little cottage all was peaceful and warm.

In the morning, the traveller said farewell and thanked the old man and his wife for the shelter and food they had given him.

44

THE MYSTERIOUS TRAVELLER

The old couple stood at the door and watched him climb the steep path. After a while he paused on the hillside and looked out over the town. It was almost hidden in the rising mist from the grey lake.

Then they saw him stretch out his arms and his long staff until he looked almost a giant, and they heard him cry in a ringing voice:

"Semerwater rise, Semerwater sink!
Swallow all this town, save the house that gave me food and drink!"

Before the old people's eyes, the lake rose up in great waves, mountain high. Then with a terrible crash the water fell upon the town and hid it from sight. The waves ran hissing up the hillside and stopped just short of the old couple as they stood trembling with terror.

When they looked round for the traveller, he had disappeared. So had the town with all its wicked people. In its place lay a peaceful unrippled lake which is there to this day.

Yorkshire

THE FISH AND THE RING

There was once a poor cobbler in York who had nine children. He loved them dearly but when a tenth child, another daughter, was born, he wondered how he could earn enough to feed his family. He worked from morning to night but, try as he would, his children were often hungry.

One day a richly dressed knight reined in his horse outside the poor man's cottage and asked, "Why do you look so unhappy, my friend?"

The poor man told his troubles and the knight listened patiently. "My good man," he said, "you are poor and I am rich. Let me have your last child and I will bring her up as my own daughter."

The cobbler and his wife felt that they must not stand in the child's way if she had a chance of good fortune, so they sadly agreed to let her go. They wrapped the child in her thin shawl and handed her to the knight who rode away at once.

Now the knight was really a wizard and he had read in his magic book that his only son would marry this very baby girl. The proud knight could not bear to think that his son should marry a poor cobbler's child, so he was determined to get rid of the girl in some way.

46

THE FISH AND THE RING

The baby slept soundly in the knight's soft velvet cloak as he rode through the narrow streets of York, out through the Fishergate Bar, and into the open country. On and on he rode over the moors and into a river valley. There he dismounted and threw the baby into the swiftly flowing River Ouse. Then he rode away at a gallop, thinking that this was the end of the child.

The baby did not sink, for her clothes and shawl held her up. She floated down the river, past willow trees and waving grasses, until the river cast her up on a sandy beach. There, feeling cold and hungry, she began to cry in a weak voice.

A fisherman heard the cry and was greatly astonished to find so young a baby lying on the edge of the river. He carried her home to his wife who had no children of her own. The woman called the little girl Alys.

Alys was very happy with her foster-parents. She played in the fields beside the river, watched her father fish and helped her mother in the house. By the time she was seventeen she was as beautiful as she was good.

One day a hunting party rode by and the fisherman called to Alys to bring him the trout he had just caught. When she came out with the fish, everyone exclaimed at her beauty and asked her father about her. Now the wizard was amongst the party and, as soon as he heard the story of how the girl had been found, he guessed who she was. He hurried home to consult his book of magic and found that it still said that his son should marry the cobbler's daughter from York.

Full of anger he asked the fisherman to give Alys into his charge to be brought up as her beauty deserved. Sadly the fisherman and his wife persuaded her to go with the knight, but she wept bitterly at leaving them. She did not like the wizard although he seemed kind and generous.

One day the wizard asked her to carry a letter from him to his brother in Scarborough, where his son was paying a visit. In the letter he ordered his brother to kill the bearer of the letter as she might be of danger to their family.

Alys set out on her long journey over the moors and along the cliff paths. She stayed at an inn for one night and while she slept a thief broke into her room to look for something to steal. In her purse he found the letter and read it. The thief was filled with pity for Alys and at once he re-wrote the letter so that it read: "Marry the bearer of this letter to my son at once." Then he crept away without wakening Alys.

Next morning she walked on to Scarborough and handed the letter to the wizard's brother. He was surprised at its contents but he sent for his nephew at once and no sooner did the youth see Alys than he fell in love with her and she with him. Next day they were married. The bells rang merrily and everyone rejoiced to see the young couple so happy.

Some weeks later the wizard arrived on a visit and was furious at what had happened. He pretended to be pleased at the marriage, but secretly he thought only of how he could rid himself of this troublesome girl.

One evening he persuaded Alys to walk with him along the cliff top. The moment they were out of sight he threatened to kill her and throw her body into the sea. Terrified she begged for her life until at last he agreed to spare her, on one condition. Taking a ring from his finger he showed its strange pattern to Alys and then threw it far out to sea. "Promise me you will not come near me or my son unless you are wearing this ring." Alys promised—what else could she do?—and the wizard returned to the castle, sure that he would never see her again. He told his son that his wife had left him, but his son would not believe this of Alys. Yet he could find no trace of her and day after day he wandered about the countryside in sorrow.

Alys grew thin and brown with wind and weather and was often

hungry. She dared not return to her foster-parents in case the wizard found her there. At last she came to a castle and was given the post of cook. A very good cook she was and her master treated her well, but she often wept for loneliness.

One day, as she glanced out of the kitchen window, whom should she see but the wizard and his son riding into the courtyard with their servants. The nobleman, her master, gave orders that a fine dinner was to be cooked for the guests and Alys set about preparing it. A man had just brought a large fish to the door for the meal and now she slit it open. There inside was the very ring the wizard had thrown into the sea. Full of joy she made a plan to win back her husband.

The meal she prepared was so delicious that her master sent for her to appear before the guests. "You must know," he said to the wizard and his son as they waited, "that this girl was a beggar when she came to my door. Now she has worked so well and my lady is so fond of her that she shall always have a home here if she wishes."

At this moment Alys entered. She had washed and put on her best dress and she held herself proudly. Wearing the wizard's ring on her finger, she walked up to the wizard and showed him the ring he had thrown into the sea so many months before. Speechless with surprise and anger, he could do nothing but watch Alys and her young husband greet each other with joy.

The wizard could do Alys no more harm. She and her husband lived happily and safely together for the rest of their lives.

THE TAILOR AND
THE FAIRIES

At one time tailors travelled about the country visiting farms and villages to make and mend clothes.

One such tailor, Thomas by name, came to a farmhouse in the North Riding of Yorkshire and as he stitched he chatted to the farmer's wife. He saw her bring in an empty bowl from the doorstep. She had put it there the night before full of cream for the hobman or brownie.

"Do you really believe a hobman will come and work for you if you leave him cream?" asked the tailor scornfully.

"Aye, I do that," answered the farmer's wife.

"Pooh!" said the tailor. "If ever I see a fairy—and I never shall— I shall put her in a bottle and keep her there so that she can't do mischief."

"Don't be daft!" said the farmer's wife fearfully. "A fairy might hear you and then you'd be in trouble. They're spiteful folk if they are offended."

"I'm not afraid of them," said Thomas, biting off the thread he was using and pressing the seam of the sleeve he had stitched on his sleeve board. "There aren't such things, that's what I say."

"The more fool you!" said the farmer's wife.

Just as it began to be dusk, the tailor finished his work, put his needle and thread and scissors in his bag and took his sleeve board under his arm.

"I'll be off before it's really dark," he said. "My wife will be expecting me."

"Here, take this with you," said the farmer's wife. "Your good wife will enjoy it, I know." She gave him a fine pork pie made from meat from their own pig.

"Thank 'ee," said Thomas. "Goodnight."

"Mind how you go!" called the farmer's wife. "Look out for the fairies."

"Pooh!" said the tailor under his breath.

Thomas stepped out briskly for his home. He walked along the lane from the farm and then climbed a stile into a large field to take a short cut to the village.

As he did so, he shifted his bag from one hand to the other and his scissors dropped out.

The tailor put his bag and his sleeve board down on the grass and began to look for his scissors. It should have been easy to find them but somehow it wasn't. "Where can they be?" he grumbled. "What's a tailor without his scissors and these were a good pair too. Well, I'll have to come back in the morning and look again."

He picked up his bag and his pork pie, but where was his sleeve board? Surely that was big enough to be found, even though it was dark. He put down his bag and his pork pie again and felt all over the grass near him. He knew the board couldn't be far away, so he got down on his knees to search.

"Plague take it!" he said at last. "That's gone now. Well, no one is likely to take it before morning. I'd better get home to the wife and we'll eat that pork pie while it's fresh."

Easier said than done! When he picked up his bag he couldn't find the pork pie. He searched half the field for it, for his mouth watered every time he thought of it, but all he found was stones and thistles.

So now he had only his bag to take home and he was hungry and cross. He went back to the spot where he had left it but it too had gone! He thought that he must have mistaken the place, but no, the rock he had noticed at the time was still there but the bag was not near it.

"If only I had a light," he moaned. "Dear knows what I shall do without my thread and needles and scissors and sleeve board."

He started towards home—as he thought—but he had turned and twisted so often in his search for his belongings that he no longer knew which way he was facing and the night was as black as pitch.

And then to his delight he saw a light in the middle of the field. He shouted for help but the light didn't move. "Hi! Bring me that light, can't you, whoever you are!" he yelled in a temper.

"Come and fetch it. Come and fetch it," said a mocking voice.

The tailor walked towards the light, but as he moved, so did the light. Again and again he came near enough to snatch it from the hidden person, but it was always whisked away at the last moment.

Thomas fell into ditches and muddied himself to the knees. He blundered into brambles and scratched his face and tore his clothes. He followed the light until he could do so no longer. As soon as he gave up the chase the light disappeared and the tailor was left utterly lost and exhausted.

At last the dawn came and the sky grew brighter. He heard the cheerful sound of clanking milk cans from the farm and he saw that he was quite near the gate of the field. There on the grass lay all the things he had lost!

He was too tired to go home so he stumbled to the farmhouse. The farmer's wife opened the door to his knock and held up her hands in horror. "Lawk!" she said. "What ails you, man? Come in."

She helped him to clean his clothes and then gave him breakfast. As she watched him eat she said, "I reckon you've seen a fairy! Did you put her in a bottle?"

But Thomas made no answer. Neither did he ever say again that he didn't believe in fairies.

EAST ANGLIA

THE BOGGART AND
THE FARMER

There was once a farmer who lived at Mumby, near Alford, in Lincolnshire. He had a good enough farm but he thought he would like to add a field or two. So he bought a piece of land and was pleased with his bargain for the soil was good and the land level.

The next day he went to look at the field and to plan what crop he would sow there first. Suddenly a Boggart appeared from nowhere; a thick-set hairy thing he was with arms as long again as the farmer's.

"Clear off!" he says to the farmer. "This is my land."

"That it ain't!" says the farmer. "I've just bought it."

"'Tis mine!" yells the Boggart, clenching his fists and looking as though he would throttle the farmer.

Now the farmer was afraid to argue with such a strong, ugly creature, but he didn't see why he should give up land he had paid for fairly. So he said, trying to look pleasant, "Mebbe we could strike a bargain?"

57

"I'll tell you what," says the Boggart grinning, "we'll *share* the crops. You'll have to do the work of course."

"Agreed," says the farmer. "When I've grown the crops, which will you have, Tops or Bottoms? What grows above ground or under ground?"

"Tops!" says the Boggart, thinking he was getting the better of the farmer.

The cunning farmer set potatoes on his land. When the Boggart came to collect his share at harvest time, only the shrivelled tops were left, but the farmer had a ton or two of fine potatoes for his share.

Well, there was nothing the Boggart could do about it, for the farmer had given him what he had promised. However, when the Boggart was asked what he would have the second year, he said he would have Bottoms. "Ah-ha," he thought. "He'll not trick me a second time. I'm clever, I am."

He was not as clever as he thought, for the farmer planted barley. The Boggart came along several times to see how the crop looked, but he suspected nothing for he did not know barley from any other crop.

When the barley was ready, the farmer cut it and stored away many bushels in his barns. When the Boggart came to collect his share, the field was bare and there were only the roots and stubble of the barley left. He had been outwitted again.

How angry he was! But a bargain's a bargain—he had asked for Bottoms and the farmer had given him Bottoms.

Then the Boggart had what he thought was a clever idea. "This year you'll sow wheat," he said, for he knew what wheat was. "We'll share what comes up and then we'll each mow and *keep* what we mow." The Boggart knew that his arms were twice as strong as the farmer's and he reckoned he could mow a great deal faster than the farmer could.

Well, there was nothing for it, the farmer had to sow wheat, but he was very worried about how much of it would be his. He went to

look at the field every week and he saw that it was going to produce a fine crop. It vexed him to think that the ugly Boggart was going to get most of it.

The Wise Man of the village heard about it and suggested a plan. The farmer rubbed his hands with glee and went straight to the village smith and asked him to make some iron rods. These he took to the field and scattered them amongst the wheat on the side the Boggart was to mow.

On the day of the harvest the sun shone and the wheat was at its best. The Boggart arrived grinning, his scythe over his shoulder. "I'll start one end and you can start t'other," he said.

They began to mow. The farmer moved steadily forward, swinging his scythe, but the Boggart kept striking iron rods and blunting his scythe. He thought the rods were tough weeds, docks maybe.

"These are mortal tough docks!" he grumbled, stopping to sharpen his scythe.

Crash! He struck another iron rod. "Plague take it! Another one!" he growled angrily, stopping again. By midday the farmer had mowed half the field but the Boggart had only cut one corner.

The sun blazed down and the Boggart got crosser and crosser. At last he yelled, "Ain't you got any docks your side?"

"Ne'er a one," answered the farmer mowing steadily.

At last, when he had to stop for the twentieth time, the Boggart gave up. He flung down his blunt scythe and screamed, "Keep the land! I won't have no more to do with it." He gave a tremendous stamp on the ground, a hole opened in the earth, and the Boggart popped down it. The last the farmer saw of him was his shock of black hair disappearing with an angry flourish.

The Boggart never came back to claim the land, but even today he sometimes pops up suddenly to frighten people, nasty creature that he is. Men say, too, that when their tools are lost it is the Boggart who has taken them.

Norfolk

THE PEDLAR
OF SWAFFHAM

There was once a poor man called John who lived in the small town of Swaffham in Norfolk. He earned a living for his family by selling the wares he carried in his pack: laces and ribbons, bobbins and needles, even tiny books for the children. He and his dog Towser were well known in the villages and farms for miles around. Towser was fine company on John's long and lonely walks and would wait patiently when his master made his calls. He caught many a fat rabbit, too, for John to take home for his hungry children.

John was very poor and it seemed that things would never be any easier, until one night he dreamed a strange dream. It seemed so real to him that he told his wife about it next morning.

"I dreamt, wife," he said, "that I was standing on London Bridge and a man told me where I could find treasure."

"Dreams! You dream too much," said his wife. "What we need is food, not dreams."

However, the pedlar had the same dream twice more. At last he said, "Wife, my dreams are so real—I can *see* London Bridge and its houses and shops although I have never been away from Swaffham—that I think they must be true. I shall go to London."

His wife was upset, but she saw that he was set on it, so she sighed and let him go. Off he went with Towser at his side and his pack on his back to help him to earn some money for food on the road. His children went a little way with him and then turned back.

The journey was long and John had to walk every step of it. He sold a few odds and ends, just enough to buy himself a little bread and cheese and ale, and at night he slept under a haystack with his dog to keep him warm.

At last he reached London and stared about him open-mouthed at the great city. He had never seen so many people or such rows of houses. Carts and carriages rumbled over the cobbles, shop people shouted their wares, there was noise everywhere. He was quite frightened for he was used to the quiet lanes and fields of the country.

When he reached London Bridge, there were houses and shops on each side of it, just as he had seen in his dream. All round him there were people, but no one spoke to him, let alone told him of a treasure.

One day, two days, he spent in this way with no luck. On the third day he decided that he had been a fool to think there was anything in dreams. His wife was right to be angry with him. He began to cross the bridge again to take the road home, but a shopkeeper called out to him to stop.

"I have been watching you, my man," he said. "For three days you have been walking up and down the bridge—you are not selling anything, you don't beg and you don't seem to know anyone. Why are you here?"

"Well, I don't like to tell you," said John, "for you will only laugh at me for a fool. I'm going home now anyway."

"Come, tell me," said the shopman. "I won't laugh at you, I promise, but I am curious."

"Oh, well then I'll tell you. I have come from the country because of a dream I had that I should be told on London Bridge where I should find a treasure. But not a soul has spoken to me until you did."

"Well, well!" said the shopman, trying not to laugh at John's folly. "So that was your dream. Why, I had a dream myself last week. I dreamt that there was a treasure hid beneath an oak tree behind a pedlar's cottage in some place called—now what was it called, a name I had never heard in my life—"

He thought for a moment and then said triumphantly, "Aye,

Swaffham it was. What a fool I should be if *I* set off to find a treasure —there may not even be a place called Swaffham. Hi! Stop a moment! Where are you off to?"

"Home!" shouted the pedlar and set off down the road at a run, with Towser bounding at his side.

John made his way back to Swaffham as fast as he could, hardly stopping for food or sleep. On the third day he reached his cottage.

"So here you are back again!" said his wife. "Have you found any treasure?" And she laughed.

But John didn't stop even to tell her his story. He rushed through the house to his barn to fetch a spade and began to dig frantically beneath the oak tree while Towser dug at his side, sending the soil flying.

"He's mad! My poor husband!" sobbed his wife.

"Let be, I'm not mad," said John. "Help me, wife, for our fortune is made or I'm much mistaken."

By this time all the children had run into the garden to see what their father was doing. They stared into the large hole he was digging, dodging out of the way when he threw a spadeful of earth over his shoulder.

In a few minutes his spade struck something hard. It was a large box. John forced it open with his spade while his family watched eagerly and Towser panted, his coat dark with soil.

"Ooh! Aah!" breathed the children when the box was opened, for inside was a treasure indeed: many golden coins, precious jewels and ornaments made of gold and silver.

"You were right, husband," said his wife, kissing him.

"Yes, my dream spoke the truth," said John.

John and his family were never poor again, but John did not keep all his wealth for himself. He gave money to repair the church and today if you go to Swaffham market-place, you will see a large coloured painting of John and his dog. The pedlar and his dream have never been forgotten.

Cambridgeshire

THE GIANT OF THE FENS

About eight hundred years ago, a boy was born in Cambridgeshire whose name was Tom Hickathrift. He soon became the biggest child in the county. At ten he was six feet tall and three feet across.

He was a lazy boy and spent his time sitting in the chimney corner. Nothing his parents said would make him work. One day his mother begged a truss of straw from a rich farmer and he said she might take what she wanted, so she asked Tom to fetch it for her.

Tom yawned and said, "Well, perhaps I will when I'm rested, but I shall need a length of rope to tie round it." This his mother gave him and after a while he strolled off to the farmer who was busy threshing.

"Take what you like, boy," said the farmer without looking. "Take what you can carry."

Tom set to work. He laid the rope on the ground and piled on it truss after truss of straw until he had collected an enormous pile. The farmer laughed when he saw it, for he said no one could carry even a tenth part of the pile.

Tom said nothing but threw the great bundle over his shoulder and walked off. All that could be seen under the straw was Tom's legs. The farmer was left gaping with astonishment.

Tom showed his strength in all kinds of ways and his fame reached the nearby town of Lynn. A brewer heard of Tom and asked him to drive a cart loaded with barrels of beer to the town of Wisbech. This sounded easy enough but the brewer knew that a giant lived in the marshes through which the road passed who cut off the heads of any traveller who dared to pass that way.

Tom was not frightened by stories of giants! After the brewer had fed him well, he agreed to cross the marsh with a full load of beer.

He had been travelling for some time when suddenly a voice like thunder bellowed to him to stop.

A giant came out of a cave. Tom was big but the giant was enormous; he was twice Tom's height and as broad again. His beard was like rusty wire, his hair spread out round his head like the roots of an oak tree and he had only one eye. He was not at all a pleasant sight.

Tom was a brave lad, but even he was tempted to run away from such a monster.

"Let's have a fight!" shouted the giant, smiling as pleasantly as was possible for such an ugly fellow. "You're a tidy fellow, not like the midgets who usually come this way. You'll give me a bit of fun before I finish you off."

The giant tore a tree from the hillside as though it had been a weed and stood ready. Tom had no weapon but he quickly turned his cart upside down, took the axle on which the wheels turned and used it as his cudgel. Then he wrenched off one of the wheels of the cart and held it like a shield to protect himself.

What a fight that was! The giant laid about him with his tree but Tom beat him so soundly with his axle-club that at last he knocked the giant flat. The giant, who had killed so many poor men without mercy, now lay dead.

Tom looked into the cave where the giant had lived. It was full of money and jewels wihch the giant had taken from travellers. Tom left it there until he could decide what to do with it and put his wagon together again and drove back to his master in Lynn.

65

THE GIANT OF THE FENS

When the news got round that Tom had killed the wicked giant, all the people came to thank him. They went with Tom to the giant's cave and helped him to carry away the treasure, for they thought he had earned it.

Tom Hickathrift became a rich man and his son was called *Sir* Thomas Hickathrift. He helped the people of the Fens in their battles many a time, but that is another story.

BROTHER MIKE

A long time ago there was a farmer who had a tidy lot of wheat. He kept it in a barn in a great heap. By and by he saw that the heap was getting smaller and smaller every day and he couldn't understand it.

He decided to find out who or what was stealing his wheat. So he got out of his bed one moonlight night and hid himself behind the old water butt where he could see the barn doors.

When the clock struck twelve, what should he see but a lot of little tiddy fairies. How they did run! They were little bits of things as small as mice. They wore little blue coats, yellow breeches and red caps on their heads with long tassels hanging down behind.

When they ran up to the barn the doors opened wide and, lopperty loo, they pulled themselves over the threshold.

When they were all inside, the farmer crept up to the door and peeped into the barn. The fairies were dancing round and round, laughing and singing. When their dance was over, they each caught up an ear of wheat and hoisted it over their shoulder.

But one fairy was so small that it could hardly lift up the ear of wheat at all and kept saying:

"Oh, how I do sweat,
A-carrying of this ear of wheat!"

When it came to the threshold of the door, it couldn't even climb over, try as it would.

68

The farmer reached out his hand and caught hold of the little thing. It shrieked, "Brother Mike! Oh, Brother Mike!" as loud as it could, although its voice was no louder than a mouse's squeak.

The farmer popped the little creature into his hat and took it home for his children. He put it on the kitchen windowsill and fastened it to the handle of the window so that it couldn't get away.

The children gathered round and watched it and one of the boys poked it to make it move. It wouldn't eat anything but only whispered in a voice so faint that you could hardly hear it, "Brother Mike! Oh, Brother Mike!"

But Brother Mike never came and the poor little thing died, so they say.

Suffolk

THE GREEN CHILDREN

It was a summer's day long ago and men were turning the hay in the fields not far from Bury St Edmunds. It was hot work for the sun was blazing down and there was not a breath of wind. The harvesters were glad when it was time to stop work in the middle of the day.

They sat down to eat their food under a tree some distance from the ancient hollows in the ground called the Wolfpits, from which their village got its name. In several of these hollows there were caves which led into the hillside, but no one ever ventured into them for they knew that the Wolfpits were strange and dangerous.

As the harvesters sat resting before starting work again, one of them exclaimed: "Who's that just come out of they caves?"

The men saw that there were two small figures at the mouth of one of the caves, too far away for anyone to be sure what they were. No one offered to go and see for they were too afraid of what they might find in the Wolfpits.

At last a boy, Dickon by name, said he would go. Like most boys he was curious and liked adventure.

He walked across the field and into the hollow—and then stopped in terror. There were two small people—children perhaps?—outside the cave, but they were no ordinary children, for their faces and hands and their bare feet were *green*.

Now Dickon was afraid, for perhaps these were Little People, fairies, and everyone knew that fairies could do you mischief if you interfered with them.

The boy stood trembling, half minded to run back to safety. Then he took courage, for, after all these creatures were small and he could see that they were frightened too. They seemed to find it difficult to see, for they held their hands over their eyes as if to shut out the sunshine.

"Who be you?" he asked. "Be you fairies?"

The girl—she was the taller of the two—answered him in a swift sentence, but to his astonishment Dickon could not understand a word she said. The boy who was clinging to her and hiding his face, cried out too in the strange tongue and this made Dickon still more afraid. It was all too much for him and he turned and ran back to the harvesters.

Soon the strange children were surrounded, for children they seemed to be in spite of their green colour. The men fingered their outlandish clothes and touched their skin curiously to see if it felt like their own.

At last one of the men took the girl's hand to lead her to the village nearby. The boy clung to her sobbing.

The children were taken to Dickon's mother until it was decided what to do with them. Dickon's mother was kind and she tried to comfort the children and offered them what poor food she had. They would not touch it, drawing away from it as if it were strange and distasteful.

It was decided that the Green Children should be taken to the Lord of the Manor, Sir Richard de Calne. The moment they appeared the village children thronged round them, touching them and pulling their clothes. Soon they grew bolder and some even threw stones, crying, "Witch's brats!" A pert boy pranced by their side copying the way the girl spoke. Her little brother screamed with fright and Dickon drove the tormentors away, for he felt that the Green Children belonged to him for he had seen them first.

When they reached the Hall, Sir Richard too did his best to find out more about the children. He questioned them again and again by signs and so did his gentle lady wife, but no one could understand what they said. Neither could the right food be found for the children and they grew weak for the want of it.

One day Dickon came to the Hall to bring a basket of beans. It so happened that the Green Children were sitting in the courtyard. When they saw the green beans they cried out in delight and seized a handful. They tore the stalks apart and were bitterly disappointed when they found nothing to eat there.

"See here," said Dickon and split the pods to show the fat beans inside. At once the children began to eat eagerly and from that day on they were able to satisfy their hunger.

The girl grew stronger, but the boy seemed paler and thinner every day. Sometimes he would persuade his sister to go with him to the Wolfpits, as if begging her to take him home. But the girl could not now remember which cave they had come from and inside the caves there were many passages and who knows where they might lead? The villagers watched the children closely too for fear they would escape. They believed the children brought them luck.

One cold day in winter the boy died. His sister wept and was lonely. Only Dickon could coax her to smile. They were often together for he was trying to teach her his own language and to learn a few words of hers. After some time she was able to talk to Dickon in a halting kind of way. He persuaded her to try different kinds of food also so that she would grow stronger. One day he saw with surprise that her green colour was fading away and that she was almost like other girls.

At last she knew enough of his language to tell him what he longed to know: the story of how she and her brother came to be in the Wolfpits. She said that they had come from a country where everyone was green in colour. People like Dickon would be thought strange and ugly, she said. In her country the sun never shone and it was always half dark and half light.

One day she and her brother had been looking after a flock of sheep for their parents when they heard a beautiful sound, the ringing of bells. They had followed the sound into a cave and had lost their way, coming out into the blinding, terrible sunlight. When they saw Dickon and the other men, all so strangely coloured and heard their loud voices speaking in an unknown tongue, they were so frightened that they almost lost their wits. Her own people were gentle and quiet in their ways.

"Where is this country?" asked Dickon. "Why is there no sun there and why are the people green?"

But the girl could not tell him.

Time passed by and the girl grew so like other people that men forgot that she had been one of the Green Children. It seemed natural as they grew up that she and Dickon should marry.

No one has ever seen any Green Children again nor has anyone found that dim land from which the Children came.

THE MIDLANDS

Warwickshire

THE KING AND THE WITCH

Many hundreds of years ago there lived a king who wanted more land, for his kingdom was small. Who could he fight, he wondered gloomily. Where was there land that he could steal from another king? He would have to be a king without too many soldiers, of course.

He called his Wise Man to him and asked, "Into which country shall I ride to win more land and to become a rich and powerful king?"

The Wise Man consulted his books of magic and replied, "You must ride into the land of England. If you can reach a place called Long Compton and climb the hill nearby until you can see the church of Long Compton, you will become king of England. So it is written."

The king, delighted, called a company of his knights to him and set out to England. He passed through the land, killing all who opposed him and burning their houses and crops, until he came to the part of the country now called Warwickshire.

It was almost night by the time he reached the village of Long Compton. The king's men built a huge fire, killed some cattle belonging to a farmer, and sat down to feast. The frightened villagers watched from a safe distance, for they were powerless to fight so strong a band of knights.

"A health to the future king of England!" cried the knights, raising their drinking cups.

"Tomorrow I *shall* be king, friends," replied their master. "We shall sweep the cursed Englishmen into the sea and you shall have their castles and lands as your own!"

Now although the villagers of Long Compton were helpless, they knew someone who was not. In their despair they consulted a witch.

"No pagan king shall rule England!" she declared. "Leave the upstart to me. I shall put an end to him."

Using all her arts, the witch mixed powerful spells in a cauldron. As the spells bubbled and steamed, she muttered incantations and traced strange signs on the ground. All night long she worked and, before it was light, she climbed the hill above Long Compton.

On the top of the hill was a great circle of scattered stones, once a temple of the sun. Green tracks ran along from many directions and ended at the circle. The hill was high and windy and, as the witch waited in hiding behind a great jagged wall of rock, dawn came, grey and stormy and flecked with rain.

The invading king and his men slept heavily after their feasting, but in the morning they rose with many yawns and began to climb the hill. "No one will dare to stop us," they said scornfully. "Look at those miserable villagers—they haven't the courage to attack a sheep!" And indeed the poor folk seemed quite helpless for they lacked swords and spears and the king and his men were cruel and strong. They stood by—and thought of the witch with hope.

Slowly the knights climbed the long hill. Soon they had to dismount and leave their horses tethered to a tree for the path was steep. They talked and laughed breathlessly, making a joke of it, for they were sure they could not be stopped now.

"Lead on, king of England!" they shouted to their master.

The king climbed more quickly for he was eager to win his new kingdom. He came up over the brow of the hill—and looked straight into the fierce eyes of the witch! She stood against the jagged rock, the wind blowing her grey hair round her wrinkled face, her long black cloak billowing behind her.

Slowly raising her arm she pointed at the king and said, "Not one step more! You shall never see Long Compton Church. England scorns a king like you."

"Who will stop me?" asked the king defiantly, standing his ground. His knights were still at some distance and as yet did not know what was before them.

"*I* shall!" said the witch in a hollow voice.

> "I'll freeze you all to stones,
> My powerful spells
> Shall turn to flint your bones.
> Thou and thy men cold stone shall be. . ."

The king's men breasted the hill and, before their eyes, the king turned into stone. His warm flesh became cold and hard. He stood there—a tall granite column.

Full of terror, the knights turned to run, but they were too late. They too became stone, cold and rigid in the wind and rain. Three knights who were whispering together some distance away, were suddenly still, just as they were, their heads together. The rain beat on their stone faces but they did not feel it; the wind howled round them but they did not hear it.

The witch's terrible work was done. With a triumphant shriek she cried, "And I shall be an eldern tree!" Her outstretched arms became branches, her thin fingers twigs, her body brown ridged bark.

There they all are to this day, watched over by the witch: strange blocks of stone weathered by many storms. The king stands alone on one side of the road, his knights together on the other, and in a far corner three knights whisper together of long forgotten battles.

Northamptonshire

THE LITTLE MAN
IN GREEN

At Rockingham, in Northamptonshire, there once lived three brothers. Times were hard and they could get no work to do and soon they had no money with which to buy food. They decided to hunt deer in the king's forest. If the king's servants caught them, they would be killed, but the brothers were too hungry to worry about it.

They made their way into the forest carrying only a blanket each, a hunting knife, a bow and arrows, a cooking pot and an axe. When they had reached the very heart of the forest they built a rough hut with a fireplace outside.

The three brothers agreed that two of them would hunt each day while the third stayed in the hut to cook any food they had and to guard their few belongings.

On the first day the elder brother at stayed home. He put the little meat they had into the cooking pot outside the hut and sat down to watch it. Soon it began to smell savoury and out of the forest came a strange figure. It was a very small man, only two feet high, and he was wearing a green tunic with a hood.

"Please give me some broth," he begged, holding out a small wooden bowl.

Instead of filling his bowl the elder brother ran into the hut and caught up his axe, meaning to drive away the little man. In his haste he knocked over the cooking pot. Although he chased the little man for some distance, he soon disappeared in the forest.

THE LITTLE MAN IN GREEN

Cursing, the elder brother returned to the hut and picked up the cooking pot. That night the brothers had to make do with what they could find, for most of the spilt stew had been eaten by wild animals.

Next day the middle brother stayed at home, feeling sure that he would be able to drive away the little man if he came again. He sat by the fire watching the stew bubbling in the pot until he fell asleep.

He woke with a start to see the little man in green holding out his bowl and asking, "Please give me some broth."

"That I won't!" shouted the middle brother, catching up a stick to beat the little man. But he escaped, scrambling and scuttering through the bushes like a rabbit.

On the third day the youngest brother, Hugh, was to stay and watch the pot. "A lot of good *you'll* be!" sneered the older brothers. "If we can't catch the little man, you won't be able to either."

Off they went, leaving the boy to fill the cooking pot with water and deer meat and make everything tidy for their return.

Now Hugh had more brains than his brothers, although he was small and young. He cooked the venison until there was a good hungry-making smell, then he carried the pot into the hut and hid himself behind the door.

It was not long before the little man in green appeared. He came timidly up to the door, held out his bowl and said, "Please give me some broth."

"Help yourself," said Hugh from behind the door and the little man ran forward to fill his bowl. Hugh waited until he had scraped the bowl clean and then jumped out and seized the little creature.

"I'll let you go and you shall have broth whenever you want it," he promised, "if you will lead me to the place where your treasure is hidden." He knew that all such little men have hidden treasure.

The little man agreed and they set off through the forest, Hugh holding tight to the hood of the little man's green tunic. They followed tiny paths, so faint that Hugh could hardly see them, and came at last to a thicket of blackberry bushes. Lifting a branch aside, the little man showed Hugh a shallow well. It was here that he kept his treasure.

What a treasure it was! Bag after bag of gold! The little man told Hugh to help himself to what he wanted and the boy did so, carrying as many small bags as he could, but leaving many behind for the little man himself. The moment he let go of him, the little creature scuttered into the bushes and disappeared.

Joyfully Hugh returned to the hut and when his brothers came back they all went home to Rockingham. They now had enough money to build a house and to buy food. Soon they found work as well and before long they were prosperous.

Never again did they go into the forest to hunt the king's deer. Never again did they see the little man or hear him asking, "Please may I have some broth." But Hugh never forgot that he owed his good fortune to the little man in green.

Nottinghamshire

THE FARMER AND
THE CHEESES

A farmer of Gotham in Nottinghamshire had made some fine cheeses and he set out, as was his custom, to sell them in the market at Nottingham. As he was about to walk down the hill to cross the river Trent into the town, he stumbled over a stone and one of the cheeses fell out of his pack and rolled down the hill.

The farmer stood and watched it. "So you can run to market alone?" he said. "Why then should I carry you? I will send the other cheeses to keep you company."

So he opened his pack and took out the cheeses and, one by one, he bowled them down the hill. Some ran into the bushes by the side of the track, some rolled merrily out of sight.

The farmer watched them, rubbing his hands. "Go straight to the market," he shouted. "I'll meet you there."

He walked down the hill, crossed the Trent by the bridge, and made his way towards the market. "I may as well have a drink," he thought, so he called at an inn and as he drank his ale, he thought happily of the cheeses taking themselves to market without any trouble to him.

It was late when he reached the market-place and he could not see his own cheeses or anyone else's, for most people had sold up and gone home.

He stopped a man whom he knew and asked, "Have you seen my cheeses, neighbour? Have they come to market?"

"Your cheeses? Who is bringing them?" said his friend.

"Who?" said the farmer. "Why they are bringing themselves, of course. They know the way well enough."

"Bringing themselves?" said his neighbour, mystified. "How can that be?"

But the farmer was not listening. "I fear they have run so fast that they have run too far," he said anxiously. "A plague on them! Now I shall have to go to York in case they have gone there."

He hurried away and hired a horse and rode to York. There he asked everyone for news of his cheeses, with no luck. So he had to come home again without them and no one has seen them to this day.

Nottinghamshire

JACK BUTTERMILK

Once upon a time there was a boy called Jack. He and his mother were very poor, so Jack went to a nearby farmer and begged the buttermilk that was left after the butter had been churned. This he sold in the villages round about and so made a living.

Each day Jack set out with jugs of buttermilk on his handcart to sell at the cottages in the countryside. One day he met an old woman on the road. He didn't like the look of her at all, for her nose nearly met her chin, she was tall and bony, and she had a queer look in her eye that he didn't trust.

"Give me some buttermilk, boy," she said sharply.

"That I'll not," said Jack. "You can pay me for it like everyone else."

"Pay for it!" she screeched. "Don't sauce me, boy."

Whee! She caught Jack up by his collar and pushed him into a big sack she was carrying.

Off she went along the road with Jack bumping in the sack on her back. As she walked along, the old woman remembered that she had left behind some odds and ends someone had given her. She couldn't carry Jack back to the town and if she left him in the road he might escape. What was she to do?

Two men were cutting the hedges at the side of the road. "Look after my sack for me," she said to them. "I've got my supper in it and I'm only a poor old woman."

She hurried off down the road. The men were astonished to hear a voice coming from the sack: "Help! Help!"

"That's queer," they said. "A sack that speaks!" They opened it and out Jack scrambled, bits of straw sticking in his hair.

"That old woman is a witch," he said. "Quick! Help me to fill the sack with thorn bushes and then we'd better all get home as fast as we can."

And that they did. When the witch came back she slung the sack on to her shoulder, quite unsuspecting. Presently the thorns worked through the sack and pricked her back. "Eh, Jack lad," she grumbled, "you must be stuck all over with pins."

She reached her cottage, emptied the sack on to the floor—and out came the thorn bushes.

How angry she was! "You wait, Jack," she shouted, "I'll catch you. I'll boil you!"

After a few days she met Jack again and once more asked him for some buttermilk. "If you don't give it to me," she said, "I'll carry you away in my sack and don't think you will escape me this time."

Jack was a brave boy. "I'll not give you any unless you pay for it like everyone else," he said.

Whee! He found himself in the witch's sack, although he didn't know how he'd got there.

But once again the foolish old woman had forgotten something and could not bear to lose it. This time it was some eggs she had stolen from a cottage garden and hidden under a hedge.

What could she do to stop Jack from escaping? An old man was sitting by the roadside breaking stones to mend the road.

"Watch this sack for a poor old woman," whined the witch. "My supper's in it."

As soon as she had gone, Jack began to twist and turn so that the sack rolled about in the road.

88

"Hey!" said the old man, scratching his head. "What's the old woman got for her supper? It's mighty lively."

He opened the sack and there was Jack, very hot and dusty.

"That was a witch," said Jack. "Quick! Help me to fill the sack with stones and then we'd both better get off home as fast as we can."

So that they did. When the old woman came back and hoisted the sack on to her back, the stones clattered and ground against each other. "Mercy me!" cried the old woman. "How your bones do crack!"

She emptied the sack on to her kitchen floor—and out came the stones in a cloud of dust.

"Plague take you, Jack!" screamed the witch. "You'll not escape me a third time. I'll boil you yet!"

Jack managed to keep out of her way for a week and then she found him again. Whee! She pushed him into her sack. This time the old woman didn't stop on her way home but took him straight to her cottage. She dumped the sack on to the kitchen floor, locked the door and went off to fetch some herbs to boil with Jack to give him flavour.

Directly she had gone, Jack pulled out his knife, slit the sack and jumped out. He looked in every cupboard and filled the sack with the witch's cups and saucers, plates and dishes. Then he climbed up the chimney on to the thatched roof and, black with soot, ran home to his mother.

The old woman came back. First she put some water on the fire in which to boil Jack. Then she tipped up the sack on to the floor. Out crashed all her crockery and smashed to smithereens.

After that she left Jack Buttermilk in peace, and a good thing too.

Derbyshire

THE LITTLE RED HAIRY MAN

Once upon a time there was a lead miner in Derbyshire who had three sons. The eldest decided to leave home to seek his fortune, so he set out to walk to London. When he was too tired to go any farther, he sat down on a stone at the edge of a wood and began to eat the bread and cheese he had brought with him.

Suddenly a little red hairy man came out of the wood. He was no taller than nine pennyworth of copper and he was dressed all in red. He asked the eldest son for a share of his food, but the young man told him to be off and even kicked him. Limping, the little man went back into the wood.

The eldest son went on his way but, for one reason and another, he had no luck and came home again as poor as he had left.

Soon after, the second son went away to seek his fortune. He too sat down to rest on the stone by the wood and, sure enough, the little red hairy man came to him and asked for food. The second son did not treat him as unkindly as his brother had done, but he took care to eat all he wanted first before he offered the little man the crumbs that were left.

"There is an old mine in the middle of the wood," said the little man, thanking him. "Try your luck there."

The second son searched about in the wood until he found the opening to the mine, but he thought, "This is only an old mine and it is probably worked out. Why should I waste my time over it!" So he went on his way but, for one reason or another, he had no luck and came home again as poor as he had left.

THE LITTLE RED HAIRY MAN

At last Jack, the youngest son, was old enough to leave home, so he set out and walked until he was tired. He sat down on the stone at the edge of the wood as his brothers had done. As soon as he took out his bread and cheese, the little red hairy man came out of the wood calling, "Jack! Jack!"

"How did you know my name?" asked Jack, surprised. "Sit down and have a bite with me. I've plenty."

They sat down and shared the bread and cheese and then the little man said, "Thank you, Jack. I only wanted to find out what kind of lad you were. I can help you to make your fortune, but you must do exactly as I tell you."

"Fair enough," said Jack.

The little man led Jack to the old mine. The opening was hidden inside a tumbledown hut. In the middle of the floor was a wheel with a rope round it and on the end of the rope hung a large basket. The little man told Jack to get into the basket and he would let him down. Then he would find what he would find.

Down and down went Jack, swinging in circles until he was dizzy. At last he reached the bottom with a bump. He expected to be in the darkness of the mine, but instead he found himself in a beautiful country with flowering trees, rivers and forests. There was a strange green light over it all, not at all like the sunlight in the world Jack knew.

As he looked round in amazement, the little red man suddenly appeared at his side. He told Jack he would find a suit of armour close by which he must put on. "You must protect yourself, Jack," he said, "for you have to fight a giant who lives in a copper castle. He is keeping a beautiful princess prisoner and you must rescue her and then return to me."

"But how shall I find the way?" asked Jack.

For answer the little man threw a copper ball along the ground. "Follow where the ball leads," he said.

Away rolled the copper ball over hill and dale, through forests and over rivers until it stopped at the wall of a castle made of copper. Almost before Jack could draw his sword, a giant in copper armour rushed out of the gate and attacked him. But Jack fought so bravely that he killed the giant. Inside the castle he found a beautiful princess who thanked him for rescuing her and asked him to take her home. This Jack did gladly and then returned to the little man.

"Now you must rescue a princess from a silver castle," said the little red man. He threw down a silver ball which rolled away so quickly that Jack had to run to catch it. Away it rolled over hill and dale, through forests and across rivers until it stopped outside the gate of a castle made of silver. Although it was night, the silver castle shone so brightly that Jack was dazzled.

No giant appeared, for everyone in the castle was asleep, but Jack hammered boldly on the gate and after a time a giant in silver armour stumbled out, grumbling at being awakened. They fought fiercely, but Jack won in the end and killed the giant. He went into the castle and found a beautiful princess there and took her to her home.

When Jack returned, the little red man said, "This is your last task. A most beautiful princess is kept prisoner in a golden castle. You will not find it easy to overcome the giant who holds her captive, but have a good heart and you will win."

The little man threw down a golden ball and Jack ran after it. Away it rolled over hill and dale, through forests and over rivers, until it reached a castle of gold. The ball hit the wall with such a thump that the gate opened at once and a huge giant in golden armour rushed out shouting, "How dare you come here, you little whipper-snapper!"

It was a hard fight, for the giant's golden armour shone so brightly that Jack was dazzled and could scarcely see where to strike. Several times he was almost in despair, but he fought on bravely and at last killed the giant. He fell to the ground so heavily that the castle walls shook.

Jack was tired out but he went into the castle to find the princess. Everything was made of gleaming gold and studded with precious stones, and when the princess ran to meet him, he thought she was the most beautiful girl he had ever seen. Her dress was of the finest gold thread and her hair was pale gold too. Directly Jack saw her he fell in love with her and she with him, for he was a handsome young man.

"Tell me where your home is," said Jack, "and I will take you back to your parents."

"I have no home and my parents died long ago," answered the princess.

"Then you can come home with me," said Jack and that pleased both of them.

"Take as much treasure as you can carry," said the little red man who had suddenly appeared in the castle yard. He helped them to gather a fortune of gold and gems and then hauled them up safely to the top of the mine shaft. There he said goodbye and they never saw him again.

Jack and the princess were married at once and Jack built a fine new house for them both, and another for his father and mother.

As for his two brothers, they rushed off to the old mine thinking that they too would find treasure and a princess. But they were so greedy that they both jumped into the basket at once. The rope broke and they fell to the bottom of the shaft. For all I know, they are there still.

Shropshire

THE GIANT AND
THE WREKIN

There was once a giant in Wales, a great tall fellow he was, who had a spite against the people of Shrewsbury. No one knew why he felt like this, but there it was; he hated every one of them.

The giant was not very clever but one day he thought of a plan to get rid of the annoying people of Shrewsbury. Now the River Severn runs through Shrewsbury, so the giant said to himself, "If I dam the river, it will flood all through Shrewsbury and drown all the people at once."

So he took a giant-size spadeful of earth—as big as a mountain—and set off to walk to Shrewsbury. Mile after mile he tramped along carrying the spade and still he had not reached the town. When he came into the village of Wellington, he knew he must have missed the way somehow. By this time he was puffing and blowing for the spade was heavy, even for a giant, and awkward to carry. He put it down, mopped his hot face with a red handkerchief as big as a sheet and then waited for someone to pass by so that he could ask the way.

After a long while a cobbler came trudging along the road. He had a sack of old boots and shoes on his back, for every two weeks he walked from Wellington to Shrewsbury to collect boots and shoes to repair at his home.

"Hi there!" shouted the giant in a voice like thunder. "How far is it to Shrewsbury?"

The giant's voice was so loud that the cobbler was nearly deafened. He put down his sack and looked up at the giant. "He's far too big," he thought. "Why does he want to go into Shrewsbury and why has he all that earth? I'll warrant he's up to no good."

So he said cautiously, "Shrewsbury? Why do you want to go to Shrewsbury?"

"Why, that's simple," said the giant. "I don't like the people of Shrewsbury, can't abide them. I'm going to take this spadeful of earth and dam the river with it so that the town will be flooded and all the people drowned. I may as well get rid of the whole lot at once."

"Oh, indeed!" said the cobbler. He didn't like the idea at all, for if everyone in Shrewsbury was drowned, there would be no boots and shoes for him to mend. He must think quickly of some plan to stop this great stupid creature from doing so much harm.

"Eh!" he said, scratching his head and playing for time. "You'll never get to Shrewsbury, not today nor yet tomorrow. Do you know how far away it is?"

"No," said the giant yawning. The day was hot and he had come a long way and felt sleepy. "Not far, I hope."

By now the cobbler had thought of a plan. "Well," he said, "I've just come from there and a weary journey it was, I can tell you. Just look!" He opened his sack of shabby boots and shoes and showed them to the giant. "I've worn out all these since I set out from Shrewsbury!"

"What!" exclaimed the giant. "Is Shrewsbury as far as that! Then I'm going straight home for I can't carry this load all that way. I shall drop it here. A plague on the people of Shrewsbury!"

Grumbling to himself, the giant emptied the spadeful of earth at the side of the road. Then he scraped his boots on the edge of the spade and went home to Wales. That was the last that was seen of him in Shropshire.

You can see the great pile of earth he left behind him to this day. It is the hill called the Wrekin. The soil the giant scraped off his boots is the little hill called Ercall by the Wrekin's side.

JACK AND THE WHITE CAP

A boy called Jack was working for a farmer some miles away from his home. When his work was done he took his wages and set off for home, his bundle on his back. By some mischance he lost his way, for this part of the county was strange to him. When darkness came he was in the middle of a wood and although he tried path after path he could find no way out. At last he lay down under a tree and, with his head on his bundle, he fell fast asleep.

He had not slept long when something woke him. He turned his head and, in a shaft of moonlight, he saw that a bear was sharing his pillow. Jack gave a yell and jumped up to run away but the bear made signs to him not to be frightened. The animal was so tame and gentle that Jack was afraid no longer and followed where it led.

They came out of the wood and saw a light shining from a small hut with a turf roof. Jack knocked on the door and it was opened by a little old woman wearing an apron tied round her middle so that she looked like a cottage loaf. She told him to come in and there he saw another little old woman standing by the fire and stirring something in a black pot over the fire. She ladled out some soup for Jack and glad he was to have it for he was cold and hungry. When he had finished, the old woman put a blanket on the floor near the fire for a bed.

"Where's the bear?" asked Jack sleepily as he lay down, for he suddenly realised that he had not seen it since he came into the house.

"That's as maybe," answered the first little old woman.

"Ask no questions and you'll be told no lies," said the second little old woman.

Jack soon fell asleep for he was very tired. At midnight he was awakened by the old women moving about quietly. He watched them,

97

his eyes half-closed, and saw that they were putting on their cloaks as if to go out.

"Is the boy asleep?" asked one.

The other came and looked into his face. Jack gave such a snore that she was nearly blown over. "Aye," she said, "he's asleep right enough."

Then each of the little women took a white cap from a nail on the wall and put it on.

"Here's off!" cried the first old woman.

"Here's after!" squeaked the other, and they both rose into the air and disappeared through the open door.

Jack sat up. The hut seemed very empty and creepy and there were strange sounds all about him that he hadn't noticed before. He was frightened.

Then he saw a third white cap hanging on the nail. Quick as thought he popped it on his head, cried out "Here's after!" and felt himself rising in the air. Away he went through the night, above the sleeping fields with their moonlit shadows. It was wonderful to be able to fly! All too soon he felt himself gliding down and in a moment he landed on a stretch of smooth grass, a fairy ring.

Several old women were dancing there, his two old women amongst them. They jigged about in such a lively way, hopping and bowing, that their cloaks swirled round them like balloons. So Jack joined the dance too and capered about clumsily until he was breathless.

"Here's off!" cried the first old woman suddenly.

"Here's after!" squawked all the others.

"Here's after!" said Jack like an echo.

Off they flew but this time they came down on the roof of a large house belonging to a gentleman.

"Down the chimbley!" ordered the first old woman.

"Here's after!" shrieked all the others.

"Here's after!" echoed Jack.

They all shot down the chimney into a kitchen, scattering soot everywhere. The room was warm and a fire glowed on the hearth. Jack wanted to sit down and go to sleep, but the old women helped themselves to pewter pots from the dresser, and crowded down the cellar steps. Jack followed them. It was dark down there but Jack could see that there were many barrels of beer and racks of wine bottles against the walls. Each of the old women filled a pot and drank from it noisily, but Jack stood by, not knowing what to do.

One of the old women noticed him after a time. "Here you are, boy," she said. "Drink up!" and she poured out some wine for him. Jack had never drunk anything but home-brewed ale before and the wine went to his head at once. Before long he was fast asleep and snoring.

When he awoke, he was alone once more. The old women had vanished and his white cap was gone. Hot, sticky and tired he crept up the cellar steps and opened the door into the kitchen. It was broad daylight and the servants were sitting round the table eating their breakfast.

"Murder!" cried the fat cook when she saw Jack at the door.

"It's the devil himself!" shrieked a young serving girl at the sight of Jack's black face, for he had collected plenty of soot when he came down the chimney.

"Thief!" yelled the footman.

"Catch him!" shouted everyone at once and they seized Jack, who was far too frightened to resist, tied him up and dragged him upstairs to their master.

They told such a tale about Jack that their master thought he must be a robber, a murderer, and in league with the devil into the bargain. He gave orders for Jack to be hanged.

The next day as he was carried through the streets of the town, an old woman pushed through the crowds and threw Jack a white cap. "Here's off!" she cried.

"Here's after!" shouted Jack, popping the white cap on to his head, and while the people gaped in astonishment, Jack and the old woman disappeared.

Jack found himself in the little turf-covered hut again. The two old women in their aprons were there as before, but there was no sign of their white caps and Jack's was gone too.

"Sit you down, lad," said one of the old women, "and have a sup."

"Thank 'ee, ma'am," said Jack. "What a dreadful adventure that was, ma'am."

"The boy's dreaming," said the old woman. "He's slept too long, he's mazed. Best be off home, lad, or your mother will worry."

"Yes, ma'am," said Jack meekly. "As you say, ma'am," and he went off home.

He never saw the old women again, or the bear, and as no one ever said "Here's off!" to him he never answered "Here's after!" but stayed quietly at home.

THE SOUTH AND
THE WEST

THE GREAT BELL OF
BOSHAM

Long long ago, when men used to come sailing over the sea from Denmark and Norway to raid the coast of England, a boy at Bosham in Sussex saw a strange ship approaching the shore. Terrified, he ran back to the village shouting, "The Danes are coming!"

At once everyone snatched up what they could and fled to the woods. The women took the babies, the men drove the cows and even the children staggered along carrying small bundles.

In the monastery, the monks hid as many of the treasures of the church as they could, and then fled to join the villagers.

When the Danes landed and scattered through the village, there was no one to be seen, for the villagers were helpless against so many strong men. The raiders carried away whatever they could find and then rushed into the church.

Now there was a peal of seven bells in the church of which the monks were very proud. They were only rung on Sundays and feast-days: ding-dong, ding-dong, ding-dong, *boom*. The seventh bell was a very large one with a deep note.

The Danes jerked the bell ropes so that the bells swung and jangled. Pleased with the sound, the raiders carried the biggest bell away with them and set it down on the deck of their ship. They would hang it outside their Chief's hall in Denmark, they thought. Its booming note would ring out grandly over the sea.

When the Danes were gone, the people came flocking back to their ruined huts. The monks went into the church which had been stripped of everything worth carrying. Then, thinking to cheer the villagers, they rang a peal on the bells. Ding-dong, ding-dong, ding-dong,— but what had happened to the deep tone of the seventh bell? They rang the peal again and this time, to their astonishment, there came an answering *boom* from the sea! It was the great bell joining in from the pirates' ship. Once more it rang its deep booming note and then all was silence. The Danes had stolen so much loot and the great bell was so heavy that the ship with all who were in it sank to the bottom of the sea.

For hundreds of years the great bell lay on the bed of Bosham Deep. Then a Wise Man said that if the people of Bosham could find a team of snow-white horses, they *might* be able to pull the bell out of the sea. Every horse must be as white as snow, without a single black hair.

White horses were brought from all over Sussex, but very few of them passed the test. At last six beautiful white horses were found, examined carefully, and harnessed together. Strong ropes were fastened to them and two men dived into the sea to fasten the other end to the bell. The battle between the sea and the people of Bosham began.

Pull! The six horses strained at the harness as the men at their heads encouraged them. *Pull!* An inch or two was gained and the men felt the bell stir on the bed of the sea. *Pull!* A ripple broke on the surface of the water. "She's coming!" cheered the villagers. *Pull!* The edge of the bell rose above the waves and moved a little nearer the shore.

Then, without warning, *twang!* the ropes broke, scattering horses and men as the broken ends whipped back. Slowly and silently the great bell sank back into the sea. Had one of the horses a black hair after all?

The bell has remained on the bed of the sea ever since but, if you listen very carefully when the six bells are rung, you *may* hear a faint *boom* from under the sea. It is the great bell of Bosham.

THE PIGLET AND
THE FAIRY

One dark night a man came creeping up to a farm to steal whatever he could find. Everything was safely locked up except for a fat piglet which the farmer was keeping in the hope that it would win prizes. He was fond of the piglet and it lived very comfortably, with more than enough to eat.

The thief, as he could find nothing more valuable, took the piglet, held its snout so that it should not squeal, and stuffed it into his bag. The piglet squealed loudly enough then but its cries of "Master! Master!" were muffled by the bag and the farmer did not waken.

The thief walked for some distance until he thought he was safe. Then he sat down on a rock to rest, dropping his bag to the ground.

Now it so happened that the bag fell right over the entrance to a hole where a fairy lived. When the fairy, whose name was Dick, heard the piglet squealing at the top of its voice, he opened the sack and asked what the matter was.

"Matter enough!" said the fat little piglet. "This thief has stolen me. My master will miss me—I'm a very special pig."

The fairy was mischievous but kind hearted too. "Run home," he said, "and I'll take your place." He climbed into the sack and waited. Sussex fairies are larger than a squirrel but smaller than a fox, so he fitted in the bag quite nicely.

Soon the thief got up, picked up the sack and walked off. It was still dark and there was no one about so he whistled to keep himself company.

All the time another fairy was following the thief. He knew that Dick was somewhere about for he had heard his voice.

"Dick, where be you?" he asked.

The thief jumped so suddenly with fright that he almost dropped the sack. Where was the voice coming from and whose was it? He looked round fearfully but he could see no one, for a fairy is only seen when it chooses.

Then, to his surprise, a voice came from the sack on his back.

> "In a sack,
> Pig-a-back,
> Riding up Beeding Hill."

With a yell, the thief dropped the sack and ran. He had put a pig into the sack with his own hands and pigs can't speak. *Or can they?* He never stopped running until he was safe in his own cottage.

As for Dick, he scrambled out of the sack, laughed, and went home. The pig was already at the farm for it had run back, squealing all the way, its curly tail curling more and more tightly with fright.

The farmer was glad to see the piglet and it led a happy life, and in due course it was made into very fine bacon.

Somerset

THE DRAGON OF
SHERVAGE WOOD

They do say that there was once a tremendous dragon up over in Shervage Wood. Its body wound in and out of the wood round about the hill and was as big round as an oak tree. Whenever it felt hungry, the dragon crawled down the hillsides to the meadows and—*glup*—it swallowed down six or seven ponies or half a dozen sheep. Then it climbed the hill again and went to sleep in Shervage Wood.

By the time folk realised what was happening, there were hardly any sheep left on the hills and when the ponies were rounded up for the Fair at Bridgwater the only ones to be found were the skinny ones the dragon hadn't bothered to eat.

So the farmers sent two shepherds up the hill to find out who was stealing the sheep. The men went off bravely—but they never came back. The horse-dealers went up the hill, too, to find the thieves, but *they* never came back.

As time went on there were no sheep to be seen in the fields, only the skinniest ponies were left and the rabbits and the deer fled to Hurley Beacon on the other side of the hill. The dragon grew hungrier each day.

Now every year the people who lived thereabouts used to climb Shervage hill to pick whortleberries to sell at Triscombe Fair. When they heard about the dragon, they stopped going to Shervage and did without whortleberry pie.

There was a poor old woman at the foot of Shervage Hill who always made whortleberry tarts to sell at the Fair. They were so toothsome that people would come for them again and again like cats for cream. If the old woman couldn't gather any berries, she couldn't make tarts and she would have no money to pay her rent. She daren't go up the hill to see if the whortleberries were ripe and if they were, she daren't go to pick them.

One day when she was feeling very low, a stranger came to her door. He had walked all the way from Stogumber, about five miles away, looking for work as a woodman.

"Well," says the old woman cunningly, "why don't 'ee try cutting in Shervage Wood up over? If the worts are getting ripe, happen you'll tell me when you come back."

The woodcutter was a stranger to those parts as he'd come from Stogumber, and he hadn't heard of the dragon. The old woman gave him a jug of cider and some bread and cheese and he went up the hill whistling. She watched him go and wondered if she would ever see him again.

By the time the woodcutter reached Shervage Wood, he had seen that there was a big harvest of whortleberries. He ate some himself and wondered why nobody had picked them.

He was thirsty too and so he looked round for a log as a seat. There was a fine big one amongst the bracken, so down he sat, took a drink of cider and got out the bread and cheese the old woman had given him.

The log started to move and squirm under him. "Hold still!" says the woodman, reaching for his axe. "Thee do movey, do thee. Take that!" And he brought down the axe so hard on the log that he cut it clean in two.

To his surprise one end of the log got up and wriggled away to Bilbrook and the other end crawled the opposite way to Kingston St Mary. The woodcutter had chopped the dragon in half!

As the two halves of the dragon were moving in opposite directions, they couldn't meet and join up again as dragons usually do, so that was the end of the Shervage Dragon.

"Good riddance to 'ee!" said the woodman and found another log to sit on. Then he finished his dinner, cut some wood and picked as many worts as his hat would hold and took them to the old woman.

"How did 'ee get on?" she asked.

"There was a dragon there at first, but he ain't there now," says the woodcutter. "I cut un in half."

"Is that so?" says the old woman and went into the cottage to make her whortleberry tarts.

To this day the people who live in Bilbrook call their place Dragon Cross, and the folk at Kingston St Mary have a story they tell to their children about a dragon breathing fire and smoke somewhere on the hill.

Devonshire

THE PIXY VISITORS

An old farmer and his wife once lived in a lonely farm on the Devonshire moors. They worked hard and after a day in the fields they were glad to sit down by the fire for a little while and then go to bed.

Usually the farmer fell asleep at once but one night the pixies chose his house for a visit. They liked his kitchen so well that they came every night. They chattered and ran about, clattered dishes, danced and made such a noise that the farmer could not sleep. He tossed and turned from side to side, he fidgeted, he snuggled down under the blankets, but it was all no use. It was only after the pixies had gone at dawn that the poor man was able to sleep for an hour or two.

The farmer dared not ask the pixies to choose some other house for their merry-making, for everyone knows that pixies play tricks on people who offend them. There was no knowing what they might do.

One night there was so much noise that he could bear it no longer. He jumped out of bed in a rage.

"What's the matter?" asked his wife.

"Why, these here pixies are making such a rattle that I won't put up with it no more. I must see what they're up to. I'll look through the hole in the floor."

The farmer crept on his hands and knees to a hole between the beams and looked through to see what was happening. He saw many pixies dancing in a ring in the middle of the kitchen and others running and leaping round them. Pixies were creeping along the shelves of the dresser and pixie children were swinging in the cups on the hooks. A fat little pixie boy was eating sugar by wetting his finger and dipping it into the bag. There were pixies everywhere and there was such a noise of shouting and laughing and running feet that the farmer was nearly deafened. He was a kind-hearted man and, as the pixies were enjoying themselves so much, he hesitated to stop their play. Then he remembered his many sleepless nights and knew that he must do something to frighten the pixies away.

Right underneath the hole in the floor a pixy was sitting on a stool on the table and fiddling away for the dancers. The farmer picked up a three-pronged fork, pushed it through the hole and made a jab at the little man. The fork went right through the tail of his coat and pinned him to the seat of the stool.

"Let me go!" cried the pixy and his friends turned to see what the matter was. To their terror they saw a giant arm holding a fork coming through the roof! In a twinkling they made themselves small and whisked through the keyhole. There was a chorus of squeaking and then the room was empty and silent.

Only the pixy with the fiddle remained. He made himself small but he still could not move from the stool and the stool was too big by far to go through the keyhole. "Let me out!" cried the pixy again and again.

The farmer hurried downstairs. He pulled the fork from the little man's coat and the pixy shot head first through the keyhole. Whee-e-e!

The farmer went back to bed and slept until the morning. Never again did the pixies visit his house, nor were they seen anywhere near it. They were too afraid of the giant arm with the fork!

Cornwall

BOB O' THE CARN

Tom Treve lived near the foot of Carn Kendijack in Cornwall. He had a large family so his eldest daughter, Grace, lived at home to help her mother. There was no money to spare for pretty clothes for Grace and she had to be content with dresses made from her grandmother's old ones.

Grace was happy enough until her cousin, Joan, came to see her. She was a maid at a big house and she was wearing her best blue dress with red and green necklaces. Grace thought she looked very fine and she began to long to have such pretty things for herself. She begged her mother to let her go out to work so that she could earn some money and, after a long time, her mother consented.

One fine day Grace took her bundle, said goodbye to her family and promised her father that she would not go more than a day's journey from home. She set out bravely, full of excitement, but when she reached high ground on Carn Kendijack and looking back saw the smoke curling from the chimneys of her home, she sat down on a rock amongst the ferns and cried.

When she dried her eyes at last on her apron, she saw a gentleman standing beside her. He was as nice a gentleman as she had ever seen. He asked her why she was crying and when she told him she was looking for work, he was delighted.

"Now good luck is mine!" he said. "I am looking for someone to take care of my home and my little son. Come with me, Grace."

Grace wondered how he knew her name and why she had not seen him coming over the moors, but he seemed so kind that she forgot everything and went with him willingly. He said his name was Robin but most people called him Bob o' the Carn.

They walked on together, always downhill, along deep green lanes edged with honeysuckle and wild roses. Grace had no idea where they were going or how far they had come, but it was sunset before the gentleman said, "We are nearly home."

They came to a green open space dotted with strange brilliant flowers and surrounded by blossoming trees. A stream ran past, there was a fountain and the clearing was loud with bird song. Robin's house was so covered with roses that Grace did not realise it was there until her master opened the door. However, the kitchen was clean and bright and a wood fire blazed on the hearth. A sour-looking old woman was sitting beside it.

"Well, Aunt Prudence," said Grace's master. "I have had the good luck to find a tidy little maid."

The old woman looked at Grace as if her eyes would bore holes through her. "I warrant she will use her tongue more than her hands," she said crossly.

A boy of six or seven ran in to greet his father. He was small for his age but his face looked like that of an old man. "Here, my little Bob," said his father fondly, "here is a nurse for 'ee who will give 'ee milk and wash your face just like your mother used to."

The old woman told Grace that she must always put the child to bed by day and go to bed herself then, before it was dark. She must never go into the spare rooms or meddle or ask questions. Each day she was to put a speck of green ointment from a crystal box into the corner of the child's eyes.

Grace did all she was told. She looked after the little boy faithfully, although she could not like him very much, and she worked hard in the house. Her master was always kind but Aunt Prudence was usually disagreeable. The days passed so pleasantly that before she knew it she had been there not months but years.

During all that time her master would not allow Grace to go outside the orchard gate for fear *buccas* should catch her and carry her away. One day, however, when he was away and the child too, Grace thought there could be no harm in taking a walk along the river path. Suddenly she heard a voice say softly, "Stop there, my sweet pretty maid, and I'll give 'ee a diamond ring." Looking up she saw a dark-faced sailorman coming towards her. Terrified she ran into the orchard. The hens clucked madly, the dogs barked and Aunt Prudence came out and scolded her soundly. That night when Grace served her master's supper, he saw that she was upset. When he heard what had happened he was angry, but he said, "I'll let it pass this time," and comforted her.

Grace often longed to look into the locked rooms, but Aunt Prudence always dusted them herself. One day she left a door ajar and Grace peeped in. There she saw heads and shoulders without arms and bodies, all turned to stone. She was just backing out when the old woman caught her peeping. She was very angry. "As you have seen inside," she said, "you may as well do some work. Polish that chest until you can see your poking nose in it, my girl."

Grace rubbed away at the long wooden chest, but as she did so she thought she heard someone cry out inside the box. It so frightened her that she fainted.

When she came to her senses her master was there. "You silly girl!" he said. "This is the second time you have disobeyed me. If there is a third time, you will not be forgiven again."

All this time she had been putting the speck of ointment in the boy's eyes each day. Now she began to notice that the child could see more than she could and she wondered whether the ointment had anything to do with it. She put a speck in her own eye to see what happened, but her eyes burned so much that she ran down to the garden pool to bathe them. To her astonishment she saw that there was another world at the bottom of the pool. There were flowers and trees and many tiny people were walking about, amongst them Robin her master. When Grace lifted her eyes and looked about her, she saw that there were small people in the orchard too. They must have been there all the time but she had never been able to see them before.

"This is an enchanted place," she thought.

When Robin came home that night, he was carrying baskets of cakes with him as if for a party. He told Grace to go to bed as he would not need her again. She could not sleep at all. Soon she heard singing and music downstairs and creeping from her room she saw through the open parlour door a crowd of little gentlemen and ladies. The gentlemen were very fine in flowered silk waistcoats and the ladies were dressed in silk and wore diamonds that shone like stars and carried fans made of flowers and feathers. When the party was over and Grace had run up to her room again she could see her master taking loving farewell of the little ladies as they passed through the garden.

In the morning Grace washed up the plates and glasses from the night's party. Her master was very pleased with her and put his arm round her to kiss her, but she said angrily, "Go and kiss your little white and green ladies. I know that you are a magician."

"Hold your foolish tongue, girl," cried her master. "I see you have rubbed your eyes with the green ointment. As you will not obey me, there is nothing for it but to take you back to the place where I found you. Be ready to leave in the morning."

Sadly Grace packed her bundle with the good clothes Robin had given her through the years. She was heartbroken to leave her master and the beautiful flowers and the tame robin that sang whenever it saw her. She did not know how long she had been in this enchanted land, but it seemed like a summer's day, so happy had she been.

At daybreak her master took her up behind him on his horse. They cantered through dark lanes for miles, going uphill all the time, and so they came out into broad daylight and the open country.

In a few moments she saw Carn Kendijack. Robin lifted her down and placed her beside the rock where he had found her so long ago. Then without a word he rode away. Grace watched him go and then, weeping, she descended the hill to her home.

Her parents were astonished to see her for they had heard nothing of her for nine years and had thought she was dead. Her mother opened Grace's bundle and found that Robin had put into it more money than they had ever seen before. They need never want again.

Although Grace often walked to Carn Kendijack, her master never came back. Her heart was in the enchanted land which she had lost so foolishly, and it was a long time before she was happy again like other girls.

Cornwall

SKILLYWIDDEN

One day a farmer who lived at the foot of Trendreen Hill in Zennor, was out on the hillside cutting furze for his fire in the winter. At midday he cut his way into a small clearing amongst the furze, thinking he would rest there and eat his bread and cheese.

Someone was already there, a little man no bigger than a cat. He was asleep on a bank of heather. He was dressed in a green coat and breeches, his feet were bare and his skin was as brown as a berry with the sun.

The farmer looked at him sleeping there and he thought, "This must be one of the wee folk. If I can keep him from running away, he might show me where he keeps his crock of gold." Everyone knows that the fairy folk have gold buried somewhere.

He put down his furze-hook, took off the strong leather glove and cuff he wore to protect his hands from the prickly furze, and put the little fellow into it, feet first, without waking him.

As the farmer hurried towards home, the little man woke up. "Who are you?" he asked the farmer. "You are a fine big *bucca* to be sure. Can you find my mammy for me?"

"I don't know whereabouts she be," said the man, "but you shall go back with me and wait until your mammy do come."

"Will you give me milk to drink and whortleberries to eat?" asked the little fellow.

"As much as you want, my handsome," promised the farmer.

When he got home he showed the little man to his wife and warned her that she must look after him well and not let him out of her sight, or their luck would be gone.

The younger children were at home and they gathered round the fairy and wondered at his smallness. He had fallen asleep again but he soon woke up, stretched his tiny arms and looked round with curiosity.

"Play with us, little man," begged the children and he played all kinds of games with them, leaping and dancing and turning head over heels in the most comical way. The children called him Bobby Griglans, because their father had found him amongst the heather. He drank nothing but milk and ate nothing but whortleberries and hips and haws from the wild rose and hawthorn trees. He was a gay little creature and the children loved him dearly.

When the children were out, Bobby sat on the woodpile in the corner of the kitchen and sang and chirped like a robin redbreast. While the farmer's wife knitted, he danced to the click of her knitting needles. The farmer and his wife were well pleased with Bobby Griglans for he promised that when next the moon was full, he would show them the spot on Roswall Hill where a crock of gold was hidden.

In a few days' time, the neighbours came with their horses to help the farmer to carry down the big bundles of furze he had cut on the hillside. The farmer did not want his friends to see Bobby Griglans for fear they might carry him away and steal the crock of gold.

The children were told to take Bobby with them into the barn and to stay there until their father told them they might come out. To make sure of the little man's safety, the farmer locked the barn door.

All morning the children played with Bobby Griglans and were quite happy. In the middle of the day, however, when the neighbours were inside the farmhouse eating their food, one of the boys whispered, "I've found a way out of the barn. Let's run round the furze stack and play hide-and-seek."

The children followed him and played quietly so that their father should not hear them. As they crept round the furze stack, they almost fell over a little man and a little woman, only a little bigger than Bobby Griglans. The little woman wore a gown as green as grass, spangled over with silver stars, and a steeple crowned hat; the little man was in a green suit and wore riding boots and tiny silver spurs. They were searching through the furze as though they had lost something. "Oh, my dear and tender Skillywidden," the little woman cried, "wherever canst thou be? Shall I ever cast eyes on thee any more, my only joy."

At that moment little Bobby Griglans came running round the stack, chasing the children. As soon as he saw the little man and the little woman, he cried out in delight: "Here I am, Mammy, your own Skillywidden!"

"Tell your dad that my mammy has come for me," he cried to the children in his high reedy voice. "Goodbye."

Away he ran and, in the whisk of a cow's tail, he and his mammy and his daddy disappeared. Search as they might, the children could find no trace of them.

So they had to confess to their father that they had lost Bobby Griglans. They got a good beating for it, for now the farmer would never be rich or his children gentry.

And no one ever saw the little man or the little woman or their precious Skillywidden again—or their crock of gold.

My tale's ended,
T'door sneck's bended;
I went into t'garden
To get a bit of thyme;
I've telled my tale,
Thee tell thine.

A rhyme from Yorkshire